Leah Purcell is an award-winning actor, singer, writer and director. Born in Murgon, Queensland, she began her professional career in 1993 in *Bran Nue Dae*. Since then she has starred in such iconic Australian film, theatre and TV as *Jindabyne*, *Lantana*, *The Story of the Miracles at Cookie's Table*, *Beasty Girl: The Secret Life of Errol Flynn*, *Love My Way* and *Police Rescue*. Her one-woman play, *Box the Pony*, was the smash-hit of the 1997 Festival of the Dreaming and has played to sell-out seasons across Australia and London's West End, culminating in a performance at Theatre Row on 42nd Street in New York in 2004. The playscript won the NSW and Qld Premier's Literary Award in 1999 and 2000 respectively. In 2002, Leah published *Black Chicks Talking*, which she also made in to an award-winning documentary, play and visual arts exhibitions. In 2002 she was made an Honorary Master of Music Theatre from Central Queensland University and the next year awarded the Queensland Arts Trust Award for Excellence for her contribution to the Arts. In 2004 Leah was chosen as an Eisenhower Fellow from Australia for her work as a Cultural Activist and in 2006 was awarded the prestigious Bob Maza Fellowship. In 2007 Leah was entered into the 2007 and 2008 Who's Who in Australia. She lives in Sydney with her partner Bain and daughter Amanda. Leah is a proud Goa-Gunggari-Wakka Wakka Murri woman.

Scott Rankin is a writer and director well known for his collaborations in both mainstream theatre, such as *Box the Pony*, *Pumping Irony*, *Kissing Frogs* and *Certified Male*, and experimental projects with people experiencing marginalisation because of race, age or mental illness; or geographic isolation in regional, rural and remote communities. These include *Happy Water Sad Water*, *The Living Photograph*, *Girl* and *Lifting the Lid*. His works have been invited to the Sydney, Melbourne and Adelaide festivals, the National Festival of Australian Theatre and the Edinburgh Fringe Festival; beaten box-office records; and received exceptional reviews. As artistic director of Big hART, a multi-award-winning arts organisation, his projects have received CHOG Violence Prevention awards in 1993, 1995 and 1996, as well as awards for excellence.

BOX THE PONY

SCOTT RANKIN

AND

LEAH PURCELL

HACHETTE AUSTRALIA

Box the Pony, written by Scott Rankin and Leah Purcell,
was presented in association with Bungabura Productions
Pty Ltd and originally produced and presented for the
Olympic Arts Festival and Events—The Festival of
the Dreaming by Performing Lines Ltd at the
Sydney Opera House in September 1997.

This edition published in Australia and New Zealand in 1999
by Hodder Headline Australia Pty Limited
(An imprint of Hachette Livre Australia Pty Limited)
Level 17, 207 Kent Street, Sydney NSW 2000
www.hachette.com.au

National Library of Australia
Cataloguing-in-Publication data

Rankin, Scott.
 Box the pony.

 ISBN 978 0 7336 1069 1.

 I. Purcell, Leah. II. Title.

A823.3

Photographs by Tracey Schramm
Cover design by Antart, Sydney
Text design and typesetting by Bookhouse, Sydney
Printed and bound in Australia by McPherson's Printing Group

MIX
Paper from
responsible sources
FSC® C001695

The paper this book is printed on is certified against the
Forest Stewardship Council® Standards. McPherson's Printing
Group holds FSC® chain of custody certification SA-COC-005379.
FSC® promotes environmentally responsible, socially beneficial
and economically viable management of the world's forests.

To Dad, Patrick, Rodney, Elaine, Oriel, Colleen, Lesley and Debra
'as I saw it'.

To the loving memory of my darling, courageous mother,
Florence Faith Chambers
1928 to 1988

Box the Pony was first performed on 16 September 1997 at the Playhouse Theatre, Sydney Opera House, as part of the Festival of the Dreaming Wimmins Business series of solo plays.

The play was:
Performed by Leah Purcell
Written by Scott Rankin and Leah Purcell
Directed by Sean Mee
Lighting design by Neil Simpson
Music arranged by Steve Francis
Original producer was Performing Lines Ltd.

Box the Pony was commissioned by the Sydney Organising Committee for the Olympic Games as part of the Sydney 2000 Cultural Olympiad and the Olympic Festivals.

The Australia Council for the Arts provided an Australia Council Fellowship Grant for Leah Purcell to develop *Box the Pony*.

Producers are Bungabura Productions Pty Ltd.

Contents

Forewords by Festival Directors

Robyn Archer

Leah and Bain talked to me early about this project, even before the team had been assembled. I had seen Leah on stage in Adelaide and thought she was very impressive; now at this cafe meeting I was immediately drawn to the strength of her ideas for the show and the great support and belief that Bain provided. I kept track of the team they were assembling, and having worked with Scott in Canberra, felt that something interesting was bound to develop. I subsequently went to the first run through in a small hall in Sydney and agreed straightaway to take the play for the Adelaide Festival in 1998.

Seeing it for the first time in full flight at the Festival of the Dreaming, I noticed how meticulously the team had refined the work since that first showing. And Leah was on fire.

I guess there's nothing more liberating than being able to stand up and tell your own story in public, warts and all. Often that can become indulgent, sentimental, angry without resolution. With Scott's and Sean's delicate and oblique touch, the story removed itself just enough from Leah's personal history, veiled it just tantalisingly enough for the performer to offer a no-holds barred approach. She came out of the corner like a winner from the very start.

And yet, the story is in many ways about apparent losers. That it is told with such joy and humour and punch makes it a tremendous affirmation of life. This is a quality I have often found among Aboriginal Australians. In the midst of the most devastating winds of ill fortune and ill treatment, there is an instinct and a will to survive that becomes inspirational—it's a belly laugh, a song and a smile big enough to light up the universe, and all in the face of the worst hands life can deal you. It is this quality that Leah has in bucketfuls—in the story itself, in the way she tells it (and the way Scott and Sean allowed her to tell it), and as she lives her life.

Robyn Archer

Sue Nattrass

When I was appointed Artistic Director of the Melbourne Festival, my earliest programming decision was to create a festival that, while providing fine artistic events and entertainment, explored issues about which I have real concerns.

The fundamental issue was equality. Having been brought up to believe that I was as good as anyone else but, perhaps more importantly, no better than anyone else, I have been concerned about the lack of equality of opportunity in our society.

One of the most 'unequal' sectors is the Aboriginal community. At the time of my appointment in April 1996 I was concerned about the increasing covert racism I was sensing beneath the surface of debate, which was affecting not only our Indigenous people but also recent migrants to Australia. Very soon after that this covert racism became overt.

The other issue on my list was violence. What is causing and perpetuating the growth of violence in our society? This question too is one of great importance to Aboriginal people.

When I saw *Box the Pony* during the Festival of the Dreaming I was tremendously moved. I was in awe of the courage of Leah Purcell, but also of the wisdom that allowed her to tell her story with honesty, tempered with a humour that removed any sense of bitterness she may feel, without diminishing the truth. Ms Purcell and Scott Rankin have crafted a play that has moments of high tension broken by wry wit and stomach-wrenching insight. It talks about racism and violence in a way that informs, without making the audience feel so uncomfortable that their minds and spirits are not receptive to the points being made.

The play's messages have been well told and well received. People who saw *Box the Pony* at the Melbourne Festival in 1998 have begun to understand some of the issues at the heart of the problems that beset the Aboriginal population and have experienced through this play some of the pain being lived by its people. I know, because they have cared enough to tell me.

Sue Nattrass

Introduction

Leah Purcell

When I look back to how this all began, I sometimes wonder whether I was big notin' myself, letting my big mouth blabber on at a pre-Christmas backyard BBQ at Rhoda Roberts' house in 1996, or was it my true yearning as an actor pushing from deep within, telling me to take on the challenge of a one-person play? No, I think I was just big notin'.

The next thing I knew I was arguing with Rhoda and trying to get out of it by saying, 'It's nowhere near ready because the bloody thing is still in my head.' But she wanted it and she got it, nine months later. I am so grateful to Rhoda for her persistence, for wanting my story to be part of the Festival of the Dreaming, and for believing in my talent to pull it off in such a short time so that I was able to perform it at the Playhouse Theatre at the Sydney Opera House.

The timer was on. First thing, I had to pick a writer to tell my story to. I chose a white New South Welshman. Why? I wanted to see what the other side of the coin had to offer this Murri woman's story. So I chose Scotty (Scott Rankin), big long bastard, he reminded me of an emu. What attracted me to Scotty, besides his unironed 1970s Hawaiian shirt, was the fact that he worked on community projects,

1

such as with kids in prisons and with the underprivileged. That made me feel comfortable. I knew he wouldn't use too many big words that I couldn't understand, and when I swore at him for whatever reason, if there had to be a reason, he wouldn't get offended by it, he would be used to it. My logic was that if he could handle those kids in prison then he could handle me.

Scott and I locked ourselves away in little rooms all over Sydney— in Redfern and Newtown—as I spoke for six hours a day, three days a week, over eight weeks. And I was sick of myself by the end of it. I let Scotty pick out the stuff that he thought would make good theatre, because that's what I wanted the play to be first and foremost. He told me his choices, I argued and asked him why, and I liked his replies. One or two things may have changed, but I was pretty satisfied with what he thought would make a strong structure for my play. During this time we spoke of the design of the stage and what we would like to use as props.

This was soon followed by the news from the producers that we had little money, and we had to choose between either a music director or a stage designer. Music had been the big push that got the project off the ground in the first place, so we went for the music director Steve Francis. Then it was up to Scott and me, and our director Sean Mee, to pick up the shortfall and come up with the staging and costumes for the play.

In the eight weeks of talking to Scott I tried to set the mood of Murgon. When we spoke of the meatworks, for example, my memory was of the hides hanging over rusted steel fences, with the blood still dripping. In Queensland, on the Sunshine Coast highway, I remembered that there were a few places where you could buy treated hides. They were actually hung out over fences on display as you cruised up the coast. On hearing this, Scotty suggested we use hides to cover the bare stage during the performance, and to represent different characters. So that's how the hides came into the play. Boxing was a big part of my life, so the punching bag became an essential feature of the play. I can't remember whether it was Sean or me, possibly the both of us, who came up with the idea of using it as some of the characters too. Sean then came up with the idea for floor matting of some type, mainly for protection because I have to throw myself around so much. We decided to go for a bright blue mat to represent the beautiful blue skies that you get in Murgon on a hot summer's day, filled with mashed potato clouds. And on the other side of the stage there was a stool to sit on for a rest and to have an intimate yarn to the audience.

The clothes racks are just there to hang the costumes/characters on when their time in the play comes to an end. These racks give the costumes/characters form and show that their spirits are still with me. I guess the racks are like a final resting place. They give the costumes/characters a bit of stature too, instead of pushing them into a bag where they will get crumpled and be forgotten. The garbage bags are the means by which I receive my 'new' clothes. The stuff in the bags represents my past, a constant reminder of where I came from.

So Scotty was then sent away to write up the first draft. I received it a couple weeks later, remembering we only had seven months left to opening night at the Opera House, and I hated it! I could not visualise the story, which is how I judge things. I then proceeded to take things out on Bain, my partner and manager, and told him I wasn't going to do the play. I said, 'I'm going walkabout, just see if they can find me!' He calmed me down. We had a meeting with Scott the next day, and when Bain didn't drop me off as he usually did but came in with me, Scotty shit himself. I told Scott that the first draft had the right structure but the stuff that filled it wasn't me. I needed to feel comfortable delivering the piece to the audience. I said to Scotty, 'You're a white male and this now needs a touch of me, the Murri woman humour,' and that's where my writing began.

Things got a bit uncomfortable between us for a while, and we had to distance ourselves from one another. This was for the best until we could see that we were both trying to make the show as good as possible. That realisation didn't really come until after the first performance at the Sydney Opera House, when the pressure of the opening night was behind us.

As it happened, I filled in the gaps by bringing myself to *Box the Pony*. Only then could I see that this was my story.

Before I go on, I would just like to say that I think Scott Rankin laid a brilliant foundation for a unique contemporary play. He gave it a style that *all* people could relate to and understand. And he captured my rhythm of words, or the rhythm of the Queensland bush, especially the south-east part of Queensland, the South Burnett area, blackfella way. But in a style of writing that showed its beautiful poetic rhythm. A very talented man.

Sean Mee, the director, was like Mr Wolf in Tarantino's *Pulp Fiction* as he flew in from Brisbane to clean up the mess. Not that there was a lot of mess to clean up. But there was a job in convincing me that we did have a play on our hands and that I could perform it. I chose Sean as my director because we had worked together in 1994 on Daniel Keene's controversial two-hander *Low*. It was my first leading role, and I received a Matilda Award for my performance. We had already built up a trust from working on that show, and I needed to feel safe in this project as I exposed my personal story to Australian audiences and then to the world. Sean was great.

I still could not see how I was going to perform this piece, and so for the first three days after his arrival in Sydney he walked the dirty old floorboards at a church hall somewhere in Newtown and showed me how my play would work. We did some editing to the script and I was now 50 percent convinced that what we had could work. I think at this stage we had two months left to go before opening night.

After that we were off to Queensland for a secret, out-of-town tryout, and to get my family's blessing to use the material. I said to Scott and Sean that my family will either hit me or kiss me. They cried, laughed, cheered, clapped and kissed me afterwards to show their approval. On the first night of the out-of-town performance I scared myself as I took to the stage. I was thinking, this is my first theatre performance in two years. When the audience laughed at the first joke it threw me, I shit myself and forgot everything. Scotty had warned me about this but I took little notice, I was big notin' again and got 'lifted'! A lesson hard learnt that night.

The show was working but we all agreed there was still a lot of work to be done. I was about 65 percent happy with what we had achieved. There was just over a month to go till opening night.

We had a few more meetings, edits, rewrites and walk throughs, by which time there were three weeks to go. We were now into rehearsal time. We were still doing some touch ups but I was much happier at this stage. I felt as if I were pregnant with this play, it was close to nine months since we started the bloody thing. We had had a few complications along the way but I was just hoping the delivery would be trouble free.

With this in the back of my mind, and feeling about 75 percent sure of things, I hit the stage at the Sydney Opera House with a crowd of four hundred people. I was nervous, to say the least. Just before the lights went down for my entrance I turned back to my stage manager and said, 'Well, I'll either see you in about ten seconds or in an hour and ten minutes.'

I gave birth to *Box the Pony* on 16 September 1997. The labour was smooth, no complications, everything went well in an hour and six minutes. The most exciting thing was the way the audience responded. They were all standing, clapping and cheering, and I didn't know why, I still only liked it 75 percent. But it was the most fulfilling feeling; they really loved it. All the heartache, the arguments and the other bullshit that goes with this sort of project were all worth it for that moment as I took my fourth curtain call. I so much wanted to call my director and writer up on stage to share in this fantastic, momentous occasion for us all.

I was told later by someone, I think it was Scotty, that yes, the audience loved the show, and they loved me too. Me? I thought, wow! My only goal on the night was to make it to the bloody end.

I wished my mother had been there so I could have run to her and cried, to feel safe in her arms, as I had just experienced the scariest one hour and six minutes in my life. I wanted to let my guard down for a moment but couldn't. I had to face the people, I couldn't show my true emotions. That experience didn't come until the final night at the Opera House when my brother and his family came down from Murgon to see the play for the first time. I raced out after the show to be embraced by my brother's huge arms, which felt like they wrapped around me twice. It was so nice as we held each other and cried, first time ever in our lives, and he said softly to me, 'I'm sorry.' I whispered back, 'It's OK.' That was all I could manage to say.

I have used all the festivals I have done since the Festival of the Dreaming to my advantage. I have looked at these performances as a way to continue the workshop process. This did not take away from my performances at all, and the audiences still got their money's worth and more. But right up until the Melbourne International Festival I was still only 90 percent happy with the show; it was the ending that always bugged me. In Melbourne we conquered the ending during a ten-hour workshop–rehearsal, twenty-four hours before opening night. We succeeded!

Right now I reckon I am 99.9 percent happy with *Box the Pony*. You can never be 100 percent happy, otherwise the play will know it has the upper hand. I've come to realise that the ending will keep changing because my life has just begun. There may even be a *Box the Pony 2* because there was so much material leftover that we couldn't fit into one hour ten minutes.

I truly want to thank Scott and Sean for their dedication to my play, our play, *Box the Pony*. I luv yas!

And another huge thank you and lots of love to my Man, Mate and Manager, Bain Stewart. Without his love and devotion, his words of encouragement and support, and every now and then a kick up the bum, I would not be here, where I am today. Thank you.

I am a very lucky girl to have three great guys hangin' around and an enormous family of, say, about…2000 (and the rest), who dearly love and support me. Thank you all so much, and as my mum would say, 'Hip hip'em Jackson!'

Enjoy! I know I do every time I step on stage.

Love,
Leah Purcell

Introduction

Scott Rankin

Leah,

I thought it was a very gutsy thing to do, to walk into a room with someone from such a different background and start talking, opening your life. Now, having known you for a while, I'm familiar with the two sides of your personality—the shy and the extroverted. I can see why there was no reluctance in talking with me, it was the performance of a natural storyteller. I was just another audience, except I was documenting and questioning and exploring. You would be quite personal during the workshop, and then when we'd finished it was, 'Bye.' You'd switch off.

The first thing that struck me was that you have a remarkable ability to recall, visually, exact details, as though events in the past don't recede or become dimmer; they broaden out as you attach other events, relationships and connections, like spinning a web. You have a gift for recognising the key elements in a story, what is naturally dramatic and imbued with meaning. These details you mull over and embellish and mythologise in the telling, so that when it came to writing, there was no lack of possibility in the material, it was a question of plotting a way through. Choosing how to discard. The material needed to be thinned and controlled, to allow it to breathe. You had a series of possibilities, and we were waiting for some

8

powerful idea, hidden within them thematically, that we could tease out to become the core of the play.

I think you're quite an arrogant person. You have to get fired up. You'd rather have a fight than a feed. You tend to crash, or crash through. I'm more reserved, and there have been a few times when I've had to sit out a storm with you wanting to 'punch cun'' out of whichever particular cun' was being a cun' and standing in your way. Occasionally that was me.

You are very driven, willing yourself to achieve, willing creative projects into being, willing yourself into some kind of new life. What life? You have no interest in 'stuff' or in appearances, maybe in convenience, maybe being in a position where others can't say no. I think part of this drive comes from being afraid to stop. Afraid to question whether people would accept you without the obvious and constant displays of talent and beauty and career.

Your restless aching drive, high-octane ambition and multiple talents rushed the project forward. With your manager and production company kicking down doors with signs that read, 'Absolutely no chance beyond this point, forget it, turn around, don't be a fool, etc', it was not a reflective creative process. It was hard in this atmosphere to find the time and the mental space to look objectively for a simple, fragile, perhaps beautiful idea, that would bring the material together. That would create a work bigger than the total of the biographical details; that was more than confession; that had a life of its own.

It's my guess that this is where another writer was useful to you, a voice from outside. I was lucky to be that writer. I was also lucky I didn't chuck it in when intimidated by the management style in the early months. I was lucky there was never a dull moment, that it was intriguing, like being in a show rather than writing one. And I think it was lucky for the project that I had the chance to be reflective with your stories.

I knew there was something out there. We scattered the burly, we had a good catch already, but we didn't have that big one, that would make it a good story back at the bar. When it first tugged the line it was almost imperceptible. Near the end of the day, thinking we could make do with what we'd pulled in, the line went slack. We sat up in the chair near the transom, staring into the deep, unsure. Then *bang*, the line went taut, the whole bloody boat was being pulled out to sea by the strength of this thing, it had a life of its own. Everybody had a go at reeling it in, you, Sean the director, Performing Lines, Bain your manager, me.

I guess that was what I was there for, to jag that one beautiful fresh idea, contemporary, unseen, muscular, with enough energy to keep it going for years. (I'm sick of thinking about ponies—'Box the Marlin', it could work.)

How you thought you could get away with working with a white male writer on a show about a young black woman and domestic violence, I don't know. But you did. That's you, I guess.

Performing Lines had heard about my work with Big hART, writing, devising and collaborating on performance pieces with people in rural, remote and isolated communities, often touching on domestic violence. They were also familiar with my work at the other end of the scale, successful, commercial pieces for solo performers (*Kissing Frogs, Pumping Irony*, etc). This combination at least got me through the door.

The black–white thing hasn't really entered into it—it is it. We write within it. I recall we both talked about whether people would get pissed off that a white man was working on this story, but you said, you'd 'just smash the cunts...' or words to that effect, so I thought, fine.

I was interested in why you wanted to write the play. Was it therapy? Was it to change things? Was it for a black audience? Was it political? Was it a crossover piece between black and white audiences? Was it for your career? Was it for large audiences or small? Any of which would have been fine, but the reason would dictate the process to some degree.

In the end it was to write a good piece of theatre with the potential to play to large audiences that showcased you and your skills, that was based in fact yet not slavishly biographical. A show you could take anywhere, that dealt with issues implicitly, was entertaining and powerful. This interested me as a writer, in terms of the progression of my own career and the writing–devising techniques I'd been experimenting with.

I love listening to candid stories told by people about their lives. I love the way a writer can help these stories take on a life of their own so they live beyond the person, and tell themselves.

The workshops were like show and tell, with me documenting. A little bit of work on the floor, a little bit of music, but mainly pages and pages of written notes. Key phrases, speech patterns, rhythms, not only verbal but the way stories naturally emerged, making thematic connections, and also looking for exit points away from these narrative connections. Some of these points came through visual things like photos, trophies, knick-knacks, and some through personal, cultural and family stories.

It was interesting to be privy to ideas and images that were very powerful, and almost secret. Ideas that were inappropriate to be used in the show. Fears, truths, superstitions, accounts of events. Together these thoughts provided an atmosphere in which to create. A whole reality from which we were carefully taking ideas, leaving others and assembling something new.

One of the difficulties of biographical material is that it is easy for the audience to be offended, or feel embarrassed at times—naturally recognising they don't have the depth of relationship with the performer that can sustain this level of intimate information. It can be like spending an hour with someone you've just met while they pour their heart out to you. An audience may even feel resentful that you are talking about yourself so incessantly—the 'so what' factor—because we all have some tragedy in our lives. Australian audiences are not 'confessional', preferring to dig around for meaning and make their own connections, through wry comparison or conjecture.

It became important to find a structure and a device that would allow us to deliver some of the story, once removed, comment on it from the outside, and return to it. We needed to create a position in which you were choosing for the audience how much we could handle. This lulled the audience into feeling looked after, and accepting the weight of the material, which in turn generated a lot of energy towards the climax.

For this reason the Steff character, as a friend of yours, proved useful. It became her story we were telling alongside yours, only to be revealed as you at the climax of the play. The use of this device created a number of problems, which were resolved in rehearsals with the director Sean Mee. Choosing to pursue it, however, proved essential to the power of the play.

It has particular importance for the white audience, because it allowed them to accept some of the horrific circumstances of the central character's story, and then, when they were already involved and longing to reach the climax, come to their own conclusion about who the central character was. At this point the power of the text surged.

The other essential ingredient was the chronology of the piece. Moving back and forward in time. Making use of your experience and past, while creating a space where you could speak to us from a position of strength—knowledge, experience and maturity.

This allowed us as an audience to feel something way beyond remorse and punishment. You were giving us the opportunity to express our own desire for a different future, for some on a personal level and for many culturally.

Box The Pony was a collaboration. First, being born out of your story and your desire to perform a piece based on your experience. Secondly, through your management—Bain Stewart, Rhoda Roberts and the Festival of the Dreaming—creating the possibility to stage the piece, then Performing Lines producing it and creating an environment in which to work. Thirdly, through the creative relationship between yourself, Sean and me. During the creative process, which continued for eighteen months, we became better and better at accepting ideas from each other, breaking away from the traditional roles of writer, director, performer. Collaboration.

Writing a version of your material for stage had to start somewhere. Before the play had a name, when the solutions were still emerging out of the fog, I wrote a first draft and nervously presented it. It was a shock. It contained a lot of direct address material, it had aspects that you felt were culturally disrespectful of important moments, ideas and icons from your life. This was none of my business, I was there to write. To look for moments of meaning and things to satirise—black or white. We had a couple of big fights. In the end, however, the first draft did set the course in terms of structural ideas and the mixing of forms for this powerful play.

It was the first of a number of crossroads in the collaboration, where you had to hold onto your vision for the piece while remaining open to new ideas. And I had to ensure I wasn't being precious about the direction it was taking, while remaining professional about what you hired me for and to fight for what I thought was essential.

The first confrontation was daunting. You and your manager don't pull any punches, and you were legitimately concerned that this writer you didn't know very well was about to tear off in a totally new and uncomfortable direction with your story. It was the first of a few confrontations that have in the long run strengthened the creative process and *Box the Pony*.

Your gifts, which shaped the writing for me, were your very strong ability for direct address, a natural comic timing and an intangible performer's quality to hold yourself in tension between high energy and stillness. I noticed these early in the workshops and knew from the other pieces I'd written that, if the material was pitched correctly, you could do three things: bridge the gap between black and white, so the white audience didn't feel bashed; pull large audiences in close to you, which is important in a solo performer; and create a sense of calm personal contact. All of these are essential ingredients in creating a good 'word-of-mouth' production, which can create strong box office. This was part of my original brief, why you wanted to do the show and what you wanted it to achieve.

One of the things I found frustrating, however, was your reluctance to satirise or take the piss out of certain subjects, especially cultural. I never pretended to be anything other than a white bloke and so there were black ideas, conventions, activities that I thought were hanging out for a bit of a jab. I'd put them in and you'd say, 'Nah,' and I'd say, 'OK.' You probably saved me from something terrible befalling me and my household.

I think a small part of your reluctance to pursue this direct address further was a lack of confidence in one area—you couldn't believe that talking directly to the audience would be accepted. You didn't believe in yourself. Acting sure, but just talking as you, nah. However as the show has continued, you have learnt to trust yourself and your insights, and the direct address is working better than ever.

We finally opened at the Sydney Opera House. It was beautiful. My partner and I brought a picnic. We sat like tourists, by the water. The angst of the first production hanging in the air, waiting for the doors to open. That day you'd gone a long way into yourself, I hadn't seen you. Cut off. Nerves.

Lights up. I sat back and watched in the grandstand as *Box the Pony* bolted out of the gate, clumps of mud flying, it was halfway down the straight before I caught up, people laughing, crying, a pin dropping. Then standing ovations, cheering. Then an odd aloneness, of being a stranger, an alien in an experience and culture I'd examined intimately, with my own personal guide, and yet could never know. Same as usual.

Thanks,
Scott Rankin

Director's Notes

Sean Mee

Box the Pony started for me with a phone call from Leah. Some eighteen months before, in 1994, I had directed her in a production of Daniel Keene's *Low* for La Boîte Theatre in Brisbane. We'd had a good time with that production. Leah and her co-star, Christopher Morris, had put a spin on the play, a kind of 'no bullshit' edge that I found deeply compelling. In rehearsal, Leah never wanted to stop; her capacity for work and the standard she constantly aspired to and demanded of both herself and the production were outstanding.

At the same time, however, she had kept her distance personally. For all the deadly dreadlocks and nose rings, Leah had retained that Queensland country reserve. She didn't dwell on herself and never felt the compulsion to tell her life story to me. I didn't feel it was my place to ask either (another Queensland thing). So at the end of the project, although we had achieved a great deal together, I really didn't know her at all. But that didn't seem to matter too much.

She was a generous and incredibly talented young woman with an uncompromising work ethic, a completely natural instinct for acting, and a quite unabashed way of pronouncing 'ask' which invariably made me laugh (one more Queensland thing). As she headed off to Sydney, my lasting impression was that Leah was a person who could acknowledge her own potential (which is rare in anybody) and, most importantly, she understood that her greatest asset was herself. So from the sunny seclusion of Brisbane, I watched her star rise on TV, content that I had played a small part in her ascendancy.

This particular phone call, then, was unexpected. 'I want you to direct my one-person play,' Leah said. 'I'm talking to some people. They want me to use someone from down here but I want you because you understand me and I want to work with someone I know, and you're from Queensland so you'll know what I'm talking about. So what do you reckon? Can I tell them I *arksed* you and you said yes?' How could I refuse?

In a rushed trip to Sydney a few weeks later, I met the major stakeholders: writer Scott Rankin; Rhoda Roberts, the Artistic Director of the Festival of the Dreaming; producer Wendy Blacklock, along with the rest of the staff of Performing Lines; and Leah. I was fashionably late, the plane from Brisbane having developed a fault, so I was fashionably flustered as well. Leah sat next to me to show that we were inseparable. They seemed to approve of me and so began a most remarkable journey.

The first draft of the script duly arrived and it was brimful of ideas: direct address, dialogue between sometimes several characters (wasn't this a one-person play?), stand-up comedy, hard-headed political quips about white people and black, an alter-ego, lyrical passages about horses and escape…there was even a suggestion for puppets. But it was bitty and the form was unclear. I was unclear. Scott was saying, it's just a starting point, but Leah was unhappy with it. The stakes were high, time and resources limited. There was a lot to do and, as usual, Leah was uncompromising. It had to 'punch their lights out'.

But through all this there glimmered a number of wonderful treasures. There was the amazing Queensland dialect, the rapid-fire string of invective that disintegrated into a throaty laugh, and Scott and Leah had imprinted that gentle, cheeky Murri sense of humour all over the script.

There was the story of Leah's Nanna, the crippled old woman who was the other person who inhabited Leah's early life, and there was her mother, so vividly drawn, so heart-rendingly flawed; a woman who loved her daughter, loved her man and loved to drink. There was the woman–child that was Leah as a young girl (that 'myall little black gin from up'ome'der'), so trusting and so unaware of the forces that were inexorably shaping her life. And there was 'Run Daisy Run', a hauntingly simple but extraordinarily potent song permeating through the soul of the play.

The fact that the play is autobiographical forced Scott, Leah and myself to be relentlessly analytical. After all, this story can only be told once. Leah knew when 'it wasn't right'. She often couldn't be more articulate than that, and perhaps that's where I was of the greatest assistance. Also, Leah was adamant that we had to be respectful to the other people spoken about in the play. She didn't want to judge let alone condemn anyone, even those who had hurt her deeply.

The central truth of the play was that although Leah's story is compelling, it is not unique. As the members of each audience engage with Leah's startling performance they are spellbound by the authenticity of the narrative. At first they are horrified, even ashamed, by the implications; the truth is unavoidable. The circumstances that created *Box the Pony* have been duplicated a thousand times over within the Aboriginal population for generations. But at the same time, the audience is looking squarely at a confident, talented, intelligent woman and they know that they are participating in a celebration, partly of her personal survival, but more because she can be actually here, telling her story.

So often this country is afflicted by notions of anonymity and the truly great Australian stories are often left untold. We sense that we belong to a society that seems to be only truly identifiable by its familiarity with other cultures. But here, in *Box the Pony*, is something uniquely Australian: the immense, beautiful, brutal landscape; the sense of space; the isolation; our ancient and modern history; our language; our present circumstances and the possibilities for the future are all at work in this play. We feel it, we respond to it and we feel stronger for it.

On the opening night at the Sydney Opera House for the Festival of the Dreaming, I was doing final preparations with Leah a few minutes before the doors opened. Leah was coping remarkably well, considering this was to be an absolutely stone-cold performance; that is, no previews, no chance to test the material; it was a one-person play, Opera House, Sydney... Anyway, Leah's warming up. She stops, looks at me and says, 'I've got to *arkse* you something. Have I got a right to be here?'

My answer was something like, 'You give a face, a name and a story to every Murri kid we see running around in those faded documentaries. You remind us that those children were never the problem. We are the problem.' Something like that.

Sean Mee

Cadence

The rhythm in the dialogue and the storytelling in *Box the Pony* is hard to communicate in writing. Leah speaks very quickly, as do many of the characters in the play. Moving from broken to Traditional language and to English creates its own broader rhythm and, off the page, the language is accompanied by strong visual clues in her body and face. To help the reader, unusual spelling and punctuation are used throughout the script to capture something of the cadence. In the dialogue, especially in the monologues, a small pause—a breathing space—is indicated by a line break, where a sentence or part of a sentence begins on a new line.

The Characters

All played by Leah Purcell

BLOKES: workers at the meatworks
BOYFRIEND: Steff's boyfriend
THE BOYS: Steff's brothers (not blood brothers but friends from the mission)
CLIFFORD: Steff's Uncle Cliffie, her mother's brother-in-law
COWS: waiting to be slaughtered
DRUNK: man in the pub
FLO: Steff's mother. Leah calls her Aunty Flo
FOREMAN: Steff's employer at the meatworks
LEAH: herself
MALE: one of Steff's relations
MISS B: host of the Miss Murgon Beauty Pageant
NANNA: Steff's maternal grandmother
NURSE: one of the Blue Nurses at the clinic
SISTER: Steff's sister
STEFF: a ten-year-old girl, then a teenager
WOMAN: worker at the Murgon meatworks

Box the
Pony

SET

At stage right there is a blue boxing mat with a heavy punching bag hanging above it. Upstage, a pile of cow hides in various patterns and colours are draped on top of one another over an unseen stand. To stage left are three bare clothes stands and an old low wooden bench. Downstage are three green garbage bags with some of the contents exposed, including trophies, photos and clothes.

SCENE 1   INTRODUCTION

House lights fade.

Music: instrumental version of 'I'm Free' by the Rolling Stones, fades in.

Light up on LEAH absorbed in working the bag, throwing punches.

Music fades out.

LEAH   G'day. No worries.

I love working the bag, its big, thick skinned and it can't hit back, just like an audience.

LEAH returns to the bag between addressing the audience.

I'm from Queensland...up'ome'der...Joh's country... Murgon...Barambah Mission...Wakka Wakka Tribe... BIG family.

Now my father, he's white. Two wives, two families, one white, one black and that was my mum. He and her had six kids together. I was the youngest.

Most nights up'ome'der—when I was little—they'd go, 'Hey, bub, come here...' They have a few drinks and then they'd all sit around waiting for me to entertain them...

Long pause.

Bit like tonight really!

They'd go, 'Hey, Leah.' I'd go, '*What?*' They'd go, 'Come here and do that dance for us.' But I'd go all myall... that's big shame job, eh! Doin' that in front of your mob, eh...but if u'fellas here want me to do it...I'll do it!

LEAH pauses, takes a stance, prepares, and then sings and dances in an exaggerated 'video clip' style that takes the piss out of her and the song, 'Kung Fu Fighting'.

'*Everybody was kung fu fighting*' shame eh,

LEAH is suddenly embarrassed, like a child.

'*those kids were fast as lightning...*'

She laughs.

> Gunnar gunnar, eh…like my mum said, you can take the girl out the mission, but you can't take the mission out of this myall little black gin from up'ome'der!

LEAH returns to start working the bag. Before she begins, she apparently catches a man in the third row checking out her arse. She clocks him, then looks back at her arse and then at him. She steps away from the bag and towards him, taking him on, holding her gloved hands up.

> Eh! What you lookin' at? You lookin' at me? Yer, I saw you. You was. Thas why you sittin' up the front here, eh? You having a good look la. You must be gin jockey, eh?

LEAH looks up to the back row, where her Black brothers would be sitting (cheap seats and cool seats), and yells to them, pointing down at the man:

> 'Hey, my brothers, this migloo fella, he lookin' at me la…' [*She points to the man.*]
> You in big trouble now…you was…knock off. What you mean no? What you don't like me? You racist?

LEAH waits, apparently observing the man's response. She then exaggerates her call to her brothers.

> 'Here, my brothers…' You in fuckin' big trouble now, they come down 'ere punt' cun' out ya!
> [*LEAH speaks warmly now.*] Nar' only jokin', cuss. So where you from and who your mob? You're not Murri, not Koori, Nyoongar, Nunga, Palawa…Woollahra. That explains it.

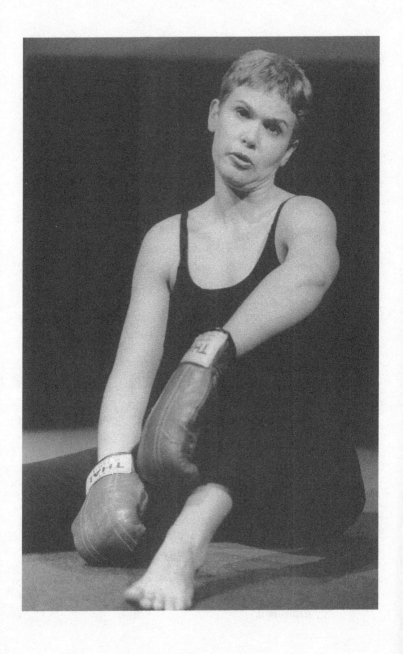

Leah moves back to working the bag.

> I come from a long line of champions.
> My brothers...Patrick and Rodney Purcell, both
> Queensland champs.
> My nephews...Darren and Nathan Purcell, Billy-jo
> Angus, all Australian, Queensland, Wide Bay, South
> Burnett, Golden Gloves champions. But Nathan, he'll be
> our Olympic hopeful!

She combination punches on bag.

> And then you got...Leah Purcell—Australian Champion...

*Leah punches the bag, it swings out and in, and collects her. She falls
to the mat.*

> ...babysitter.
> I wasn't allowed to box, because I was a girl. Up'ome'der,
> all the girls got to do was cook, clean and look after the
> kids.
> The boys got all the deadly things, the trophies, the
> Golden Gloves...
> The brain damage.

Combination punches on the bag.

> Fighting was big up'ome'der...people would fight like
> hell.
> But the men and the women would fight differently. With
> the men it was all piss and wind.

*Leah drops her gloved hands, pushes out her chest, stands on her toes
and looks down her nose at her opponents. She is bumping chest bones*

*against the other imaginary person (symbolised by the punching bag) as
they try to push each other back.*

> 'Yeah, come on, I'll fight ya.
> Yeah, yeah!'
> But with the women, they wouldn't say a word…they
> just clock ya, dress tucked up in the undies…and it
> was on.

*Leah clocks her female opponent, lifts the side of her skirt up and tucks
it into her undies.*

She says to the woman on the ground, whom she has just flattened:

> 'Come on, get up!'
> That's how it was in Murgon. You learnt to fight to
> impress people…or you learnt how to bullshit to them.
> And bullshitting is basically what I'll be doing here
> tonight.

Big smile. She moves to the garbage bags, taking off her gloves.

Scene 2   LEAH IN SYDNEY

LEAH starts to walk downstage to the garbage bags to collect her cap and jumper.

LEAH   When I grew up, I took off from up'ome'der. I grabbed the essentials…

She puts on a landrights jumper and cap.

And jumped in my little yellow Datsun Sunny…[*sings*] '*Sunny, thank you for the smile upon my face…*'

LEAH sings while she physicalises driving a car. Using the steering wheel, she reaches up to adjust the rear-view mirror and it falls off in her hand. She throws it into the back seat.

Good car. Straight to Sydney, Eastern Suburbs, real flash. Had to live somewhere, right? So I go to a real estate agent.

'G'day'…and true's god, the woman behind the counter looks at me and says, 'We haven't any money, we haven't any money, take whatever you want.'

So I took a one-bedroom flat.

See, blackfella not greedy.

So now I live in Woollahra, real fuckin' flash, which is nice…because as Aunty Pauline Hanson says, 'Too many people up'ome get paid too much money for sitting around drinking too much port.' So Woollahra feels like home.

Then I get this job presenting on cable TV and all of a sudden I'm a BIG star in Woollahra! Solid, eh?

But serious now…them fellas in Sydney they different

LEAH (cont'd)   mob, eh? Up'ome'der when you drivin' and a car passes,
                       you wave.

LEAH waves to a passing car while singing 'Sunny'.

She says to a passing car:

                       'Hey, cuss.'
                       But here in Sydney, biggest mob of bloody cars, I'm
                       wavin' all bloody day, what's wrong with them fellas?
                       None of them bastards wave back!

*LEAH sits on the bench as though she is in a park and someone is sitting
next to her. She talks to them.*

                       And another thing, you're sitting next to someone.
                       'G'day.' 'Where you come from?' 'Woollahra?' 'Hey, you
                       and me and this bloke over here, same mob. We'll have
                       to get together and have a cup of tea.'
                       'I'm from up'ome'der,
                       'Murgon.'
                       'My father he's white, two wives, two families, one white
                       and one black…and…that…was…my mum.
                       'Here, where you goin'?'
                       'It gets better!
                       'I haven't got up to the part about me being conceived
                       at the dump!'

*LEAH is surprised when the person gets up and leaves in a hurry, while
she is talking.*

                       'Suit yourself…'
                       Another time, I'm walking down the street and this lady
                       comes out of her gate and, true's god, it's like a bloody
                       cartoon. She grabs her bag and goes…

As WHITE WOMAN frightened by seeing a blackfella up close, she clutches her handbag to her chest and blinks, stopping in her tracks as if she fears LEAH might hit her.

> like I was going to hit her or something…

LEAH visualises the garden path, front door and hall by crouching and looking way into the back of the stage. She becomes the woman backing away and rolling in a backward somersault up the hall in slow motion as she speaks.

> She backs in her gate, up the path, falls in the front door, rolls up the hallway, doing backward somersaults… [*somersault*]…slow motion…[*somersault*].

As LEAH, she walks back to her starting point and watches where the woman has gone.

> And I stood there thinking…
> Shit, I better get back to the story. Come on, serious now.

LEAH takes off her landrights jumper and cap. The music to the song 'Run Daisy Run' begins. She moves into choreography for the song.

During the song a large projected image of a wise elderly Black woman's eyes fades in, upstage.

Into dance routine for 'Run Daisy Run'.

SCENE 3   RUN DAISY RUN

LEAH   *Wondah yarrmun taia nunni kurra mulli kai ngun ngun tulla yani yani.*

The winds they don't blow any more,
Fields are empty and bare.
The children, they don't play.
The mummas they are weeping,
The children can't be heard
They will never meet again.

She heard, 'Run Daisy run, run Daisy run,'
They were the last words her mama had said.
'Run to the highlands, run through the scrub,
'Just run, run Daisy run, just run, just run,
Because the whiteman he's ridin' high.'

She was just a little girl, indigenous to this land,
She was happy, she was home, had her family never alone.
But then the day came, her tribal wind has gone
The spirits howl of sorrow, the white man on horseback he came,
To take the children away.

Treated like animals children chained all fours
They walked many a mile in a day
Most of then reached the destination but a lot were left on the road
She never...no never...saw her mama again.

LEAH (cont'd) *She heard, 'Run Daisy run, run Daisy run.'*
They were the last words her mama had said.
'Run to the highlands, run through the scrub,
You just gotta run, run Daisy run, just run, just run.
Because the whiteman, he's ridin' high.'

Wondah yarrmun taia nunni kurra mulli kai ngun ngun tulla
yani yani. [repeat]

(Whiteman on horseback come and took my baby, where all
I can do is cry.)

Scene 4   THE EARLY YEARS

Leah moves to the garbage bags, looks through them and finds Steff's small yellow summer dress.

Holding the dress up so she is looking at it and then at the audience, she swirls around, moving upstage.

LEAH   Up'ome'der, there was this girl called Steff, my little tidda der, myall little black gin from up'ome'der, gunnar, gunnar, all she wore was a little hand-me-down frock and a couple of love bites.
And all them boys they be lookin' at her and say to each other...

THE BOYS Oohh...come on, stuck right in, balls and all...oohh... You wish...Yer last night I was there...You wasn't... Yeah?...Yeah!

STEFF   Oh, go way...in ya dreams.

Leah puts Steff's dress on, picks up the top cow hide on the pile and flings it out so it spreads in the air and falls flat on the ground. As it lands, Leah steps onto it and, in that step, becomes Steff. (The hides take on characters in Leah's life.)

LEAH   Steff was just a normal kid...her and her friends played dress-ups together...pretend games together...got pregnant, except they were pretending.
She was pretty pissed off about that.
She went to the Blue Nurses at the clinic.

Leah becomes the nurse, looking down at Steff.

NURSE   Ohhrr, what's the matter, bub, you poxed up or what?

NURSE (cont'd) You this way you gundaburri. But you too young, eh? 'Ere Steffie, what you want a little boy or little girl?

LEAH becomes STEFF, myall, looking up at the NURSE.

STEFF Um...a pony?

LEAH She was mad for them bloody horses.

LEAH throws the second cow hide onto the ground. It represents the character of NANNA.

Steff was Bungabura. When she was little her nanna called her that, Gamilaroi for blue crane...that's a bird from up'ome'der.

LEAH takes on the form of the blue crane.

Got these long legs...and long neck...and a soulful cry.

LEAH dances as the blue crane.

STEFF Nanna can't do this no more. Arthritis got her real bad.

She dances over to NANNA's hide.

LEAH Steff'd play tricks on Nanna, like move her bedpan out of reach. Pretty stupid really, because she had to clean it up.
Her nanna couldn't walk. Could hardly move, bedridden, Steff had to look after her.

LEAH moves between being NANNA, shrivelled up with arthritis, and STEFF watching 'Neighbours' on TV. She moves rhythmically, stepping between their two hides to play each character. The movement is dance-like and the following words are delivered with the same rhythm.

NANNA   Water…water.

STEFF is watching 'Neighbours', humming and singing part of the theme song.

STEFF   What?

NANNA   Water…

STEFF   Yeah, wait there, Nanna Daisy…

NANNA   Water.

STEFF   Ad break soon. Hold your horses, Daisy Duck.

NANNA   Water.

STEFF   Nanna!

STEFF is annoyed that NANNA has interrupted her TV, and gets up to get her a water.

             Eh, Nanna…I gotta go up 'ere…see Mum up the pub there.

NANNA, crippled by arthritis, has her head down.

NANNA   Here girl, they there for you. In the backyard… Bungabura, you gonna be tall like them blue cranes. You gotta fly away girl, you run away.

LEAH   Steff's nanna couldn't have known the blue cranes were there. She couldn't move…

NANNA   What's your name, girl?

STEFF has become afraid of the respect for NANNA's spiritual insight.

STEFF   Um, Bungabura…I got to go, Nanna. Pension day…see
              Mum at the pub der.

*STEFF runs from NANNA, in fear. Moving behind the punching bag she
becomes LEAH.*

LEAH   Another time, up at the pub, Steff sees her mum on the
              verandah, talking to an old man on a pony…

STEFF   Old fella, white hair all swept back, solid!
              [*sniffs*] Horse and Brylcream.
              Black man dressed real deadly like John Wayne. Cowboy
              coat and shiny boots. Must be real important. One of
              them Government blackfellas.

LEAH   He was her grandfather. A drover. He's retirin' soon and
              that horse will be glue.

*STEFF looks at the horse, moves slowly towards it, nervous. She puts one
hand under its chin and strokes its head with the other.*

STEFF   That pony, he clocked me, eh. He looking me over *real*
              slow. He winking at me, eh. Mum don't see. That pony
              he saying something to me. I can hear him, eh.
              He sayin', 'Help me, save me, ask your mum!'

SCENE 5   STEFF'S MUM

A country version of the song 'Jackson' is playing. LEAH hangs up STEFF's dress and then, looking in the garbage bags, she finds a large pink floral sun frock, which she holds up.

LEAH   Steff's mum. Florence. Big woman.

LEAH puts the dress on.

             Every second Thursday, Steff's mum'd dress up.

LEAH mimes putting on lipstick as if she is preparing for a day out.

FLO   I've got a date with Don. Don Camillo, Spumante.

LEAH   She heads off. Up town. Bank first…

Throws a cow hide over the wooden bench to represent the character of STEFF's mother.

             because it's pension day.
             Steff cuts from school, to catch her up.

LEAH throws down a smaller hide (similar to STEFF's first hide) to represent STEFF at a younger age.

             Most blackfellas weren't allowed in the pub. Drink on
             the footpath. But Florence was allowed in. Cleaned for
             some white people…she's a respectable woman.

FLO   [*To STEFF*] You right bub? Got your cherry cheer and
             chips?

While sitting on the hide covering the bench (symbolising sitting at the bar at the pub), FLO sees a friend at the door. She signals for him to come in and join her. The friend is obviously nervous about coming in.

Eh country! Come here, boy! Come here.

She signals to the barman.

It's right, hey Jackson?
[*Speaking to the friend at the door*] Country, come here. Where you going? Come and have a charge with Aunty Flo. You right, you with me. But like I tell all these fellas, you muck up. Here! Knock off! My shout, eh?

LEAH   Pub would start jumping. Aunty Flo be big notin'.

FLO   I'm just going to the powder room, powder my nose.

FLO begins to walk off, moving her hips in an exaggerated way.

MALE   Hey, Aunty! Thas not your walk!

She turns back playfully.

FLO   Ahh…that's my walk! Gorn you don't know.
               Hip hip'em Jackson.

She waddles off.

LEAH   Steff'd be under the table. She's listening and looking. Everybody's charged up.

MALE   Hey, Steffie bub, come out here and do that dance for us.

STEFF   Piss off, dickhead. Mum, I wanna go home.

STEFF looks for her mother.

FLO   'Ere hang on bub, here look what I got here. Steff come
                 and have a dance with Mum.

*FLO puts a bottle top under each foot and presses down so they stick to
the soles of her feet. She exaggerates a tap routine to 'Jackson', which
has continued to play in the background.*

*Volume up for tap dancing. FLO sings along to the words of 'Jackson'
and claps, having a good time.*

                 Come on bub, come and dance with your mother.

It's now evening, STEFF is sitting under the table, getting tired and bored.

STEFF   Mum…Mum. I'm hungry, I want a feed!

FLO has been drinking for some hours.

FLO   Hey! 'Ere bub, you forgot about Nanna. You better go
                 and give her a feed, eh? Put Nanna on the pot. Gorn,
                 gorn bub. What's the matter? You go home and fry up
                 some eggs. You have a feed, then come straight back.
                 Gorn now.

End of music under: 'Jackson'.

LEAH   Two eggs, two pieces of burnt toast swimming in tomato
                 sauce. She tried her best. She was only ten.

The tomato sauce splatters, she carries the food to NANNA, STEFF's upset.

NANNA   What you cryin' for, bub?

*NANNA, shrivelled and stiff with arthritis and shaking, gathers STEFF (the
first hide represents STEFF) to her.*

> Ooh come here, bub. Come here to Nanna. Don't cry,
> Bungabura, We have a story eh? This good food.
> When I was little we only had water and potatoes. I
> asked them old people on Barambah Mission, I say,
> where I come from? They say, migloo wondah he took
> me when I was little joujin, tulla. I yanni, yanni all the
> time for my ngumba and buba. No more, all gone, tulla?
> Put me on big train, went for long time, up and down,
> up and down, more little joujins. They yanni, yanni all
> the time too.
> New home land now. Tin yumba, dirt floor…ooh but he
> spotless clean, here sssshhh…bossman, bulliman comin'
> …top camp, middle camp, bottom camp. I'm middle
> camp Murri woman now. Corroboree every Friday night.
> Good times, sad times…hard times…

*She says lines of Gunggari language Gamilaroi dialect from 'Run Daisy
Run'.*

> 'Wondah yarrmun taia nunni kurra mulli kai ngun ngun
> tulla yani yani.'
> I'm gunggari umbi…Here bub, what's your name? Come
> on, tell Nanna. You say it now, gorn.

STEFF   Bungabura

NANNA   You fly away!

*STEFF leaves. Background music, 'Jackson', plays. We are back in the
pub. FLO is now very drunk.*

FLO   Hey! Where you been bub, eh? Come here and dance
           with your mother!

STEFF   Mum, I'm tired. Got school tomorrow. Don't be sittin'
           there bein' stubborn. Mum, I wanna go home!

FLO   You just wait there!
           Wait there! I can't be goggling my drink.

*FLO sits with her back to the audience and slowly finishes her drink. She
is very drunk, almost falling asleep and mumbling to herself in a
stubborn way about not wanting to be rushed. She drinks three times,
putting the glass back on the table between each. Each sip is sleepier
than the one before. At last she falls asleep, with her head coming to
rest on her bosom.*

FLO wakes with a start and stands.

           Alright, let's go. 'Ere bub, carry the baby.

Mime: FLO hands STEFF a carton of XXXX.

LEAH   She gives Steff the baby—a carton of XXXX—and invites
           everybody up'ome for a party.
           Outside some old whitefella is sniffing around. Steff
           clocks him, she knew.

STEFF   Eh! Fuck off!

DRUNK   You got a bad mouth on you girlie.

STEFF   Yeah, it's for arseholes like you. So sit and spin fuck
           knuckle!

FLO   Hey! Knock off talking like that.
               I'm a grown woman. My house, I pay the bills. I'm a
               grown woman. Anyway, it's my party and, you know
               what, he can come.

Party begins with trail end of 'Jackson' by Rogers and Wheeler.

FLO continues to sing and move.

LEAH   Everybody's in the kitchen, partying up…

Song: 'Rockin' All Over the World' by Status Quo.

               There's a hell of a racket…

Song: 'I Can't Stop Loving You' by Tom Jones.

               Steff's out in the hallway, she's curled up, she's tired, but
               she's listening.

Song: 'I Want to Break Free' by Queen.

FLO   [*Singing along to the song*] When I'm dead and gone bub
               don't you cry for me, don't you cry.

LEAH   When they drift home, Aunty Flo gets out the old 45s.
               If it's Elvis, she's happy. But if it's Roy Orbison, she'd
               be there in the lounge room in the dark, bawling her
               eyes out.

Song: 'Leah' by Roy Orbison.

FLO   'Leah, Leah. Here I go from the hut to the sea for Leah.'

FLO falls drunk.

STEFF   Mum…turn it down a bit.

FLO   Come here, my daughter. Come and dance for Mama.
                 I'm sorry.
                 Do you forgive me?
                 Here, bub, put Mum to bed.

*FLO pulls STEFF's smaller cow hide to her and holds it close, they move
to the music. FLO is tired. LEAH takes off FLO's dress and lays it down
with the hide.*

LEAH   Steff slept in the same bed as her mum until she was
                 fourteen. But she didn't sleep much when her mum was
                 drunk.
                 Steff thought her mum might die.

STEFF   [*whispers*] Mum…mum…you breathin'…?

*Music under with a rhythmic, free wild drumming. Music for the pony
and STEFF's escape.*

LEAH   Just on daybreak, she hears it. Outside the window, her
                 grandfather's pony. Cropping grass, breathing, the shake
                 of a mane, the clink of the bridle. She smells the dew
                 on his hide. He's there for her.

The music continues under and becomes the song, 'Horse Hair'.

SCENE 6   HORSE HAIR

LEAH   *A blur of ditches and fallen grey trees, a flick of wind and*
I'm clutching your horse hair.
Over the ground it's the colour of mustard, takes me bolting
under hanging bark of trees.

I hear the whispers, save me, *I hear the whispers,* save me
now.
I hear the whispers, save me, *I hear the whispers,* save me
now.

And I feel whipping grass on my ankles, wind in my mouth
dries my silent tongue.
Pounding and pounding my heart and your hooves, take me
bolting into the bluest sky.

I hear the whispers, save me, *I hear the whispers,* save me
now
I hear the whispers, save me, *I hear the whispers,* save me
now.

Bare face and bare feet and bare back, don't take me back
there.
Bare skinned and laid bare and bare back, don't take me
back there.

Your wild scented flesh is foaming my eyes and ears I feel
I'm inside you.
My summer hand-me-down is blowing floral pleats against
the bluest Queensland sky.

I hear the whispers, save me, *I hear the whispers,* save me
now
I hear the whispers, save me, *I hear the whispers,* save me
now.

Scene 7   DOING COFFEE IN SYDNEY

Leah sitting on the wooden bench.

LEAH   Now where was I?

Sydney, Woollahra. I'm fitting in. [*Sees a passing car, waves.*] Porsche. [*Sees another, waves.*] Merc. [*And another, waves.*] Audi…Datsun Sunny Deluxe 1000 1971. 'Hey cuss!' [*Big, big wave.*]

They're still not waving!

In Woollahra, people do coffee on the footpath. Now this is hard for a little myall black gin to understand. Because up'ome'der you drink on the footpath because you're not allowed into the pub.

These gubba fellas just don't do coffee on the footpath, their dogs, which they treat like children, do gunung!

Wiping feet as if having trodden in gunung.

That's filthy. That's stinkin', thas dirty that! And they got a cheek to say blackfella dirty!

One time, I see this woman doing coffee and pancakes, and I recognise her…she's the woman who somersaulted in scene one. And I'm thinking, white woman can't be wandering around in my story! That's cultural imperialism! That's bloody racist!

She recognises me and she sniffs like this…

Sniffing as snobby white woman.

Funny that because that gunung don't seem to worry her. I go like this [*wave friendly*] and she goes like this…

Scared, with her hands pulled up to her chin over her cup of coffee.

LEAH (cont'd)   and one of her gold rings slips off and falls into the froth
                     of her cappuccino. Clink!

Miming the action.

> She goes in to get it, first with her fingers, and then with
> her arm. She loses her grip and she falls in. She's
> wearing so much gold, she starts to sink. And she's
> yelling, 'Help me, help me!'
> I'm thinkin' she's going to drown so I reach in, but she
> goes…

Barking.

> and swims away. And she swims round and around, the
> froth begins to churn. She goes faster and faster and the
> milk starts to thicken…faster and faster and thicker and
> thicker…and all of a sudden she's gone.
> And all that's left is this lovely cup of delicious yellow
> butter.

*Leah looks at the butter and pancakes, and then looks around to see if
anyone is watching.*

> And I'm thinkin', hey, this good food,
> can't be wastin', so I get stuck into it!

*Leah quickly mimes buttering a pancake and then eating it. She slowly
becomes aware of the taste and stops.*

*Looking at the pancakes on the table and then at a woman in the
audience she says:*

> You white woman *are* salty.
> Then I see the woman's handbag. It's a $3000 Chanel,

LEAH (cont'd)   real fuckin' flash one. That's a deposit on a house
                     up'ome'der.

She picks it up, then sees someone close by.

                     [*To the woman*] 'Here, Aunty!' [*To the audience*] Bag lady
                     collecting cans. [*To AUNTY*] 'Here Aunty, it's yours, you sell
                     it and you won't be poor.' [*To audience*] Then get this!
                     You know what she said to me? 'What would a rich bitch
                     like you know about poverty?'
                     Jesus, a couple of lo-cal, high-fibre pancakes and a skim-
                     milk cappuccino and my cultural identity is washed
                     away. Maybe it's true. You are what you eat!
                     Eeeeeeeeooooo, the butter!

She spits out the food…

                     And I say to her, 'I know what poor is. There is a higher
                     infant mortality amongst kids up'ome'der than among
                     puppies in Woollahra. They got more vets here than we
                     got dogs! So don't tell me I don't know what poor is!'

LEAH climbs up on the wooden stool, raising her fist in the air.

                     So I'm up and I'm about to claim native title over the
                     whole of the Eastern Suburbs…when the bag lady
                     hands me a note…

She takes a note from the woman and reads it.

                     'Dear Leah, get off the soap box. Forget the Woollahra
                     thing. This is not political theatre. Get back to the story.'

SCENE 8   MISS MURGON

LEAH   In 1987, Steff was fifteen. The biggest time of the year
             in Murgon was the Agricultural Show…gave the farmers
             the opportunity to show off their livestock. You got the
             chooks…*brrk, bbrkk*…the bulls…*mmmmmhhh*, and
             then their daughters…

LEAH takes a purple 1980s evening dress out of one of the plastic bags.

             the Beauty Pageant.

Puts on the purple Miss Murgon dress.

             First prize Miss Agricultural Show, second prize was
             Miss Murgon and third prize Miss Tragic.

MISS B   [*posh*] Ladies and Gentlemen, entrant number 11.
             Stephanie's goals include: starring in the high-school
             musical, making the Wide Bay Netball team, and
             completing grade ten.

LEAH gives a look that says 'No chance!'.

LEAH   Like all the girls, Steff went to Miss Bowman's
             deportment and grooming class, where they taught you
             how to…

Walks like a model centre stage towards audience.

             walk up and down, spin on a sixpence…

Spins and nearly falls over.

LEAH (cont'd)   and make a bloody fool out of yourself.

> *LEAH moves to the punching bag, as though she is waiting in the wings at the Beauty Pageant. The boxing bag becomes the other girl, MISS TRAGIC.*

> You had to make a speech, and Steff, being the little myall black gin from up'ome'der, Miss Bowman said she would help her choose the topic. So Steff's in the wings waiting her turn and that Miss Tragic bitch keeps bumping into her.

STEFF   [*To bag*] Knock off or I'll flatten ya, ya cheeky bitch!

> *STEFF is about to hit MISS TRAGIC when she hears the announcement.*

LEAH   Over the PA Steff hears Miss Bowman. 'Stephanie will speak on "Racial Harmony in Strife-torn Regional Australia"…'

> *STEFF hits MISS TRAGIC and motions for her to get up (fighting like women).*

STEFF   Get up!

> *Walks out on high heels as STEFF, while speaking as LEAH.*

LEAH   So Steff totters out in her high heels…her mob is there, up the back six tables full. And they're all goin' 'Woo yeah alright!'

> *STEFF waves to her mob and then speaks formally, as if at a microphone.*

STEFF   Racial harmony…Racial harmony requires both parties…

LEAH   Bugger me dead, her mob up the back start a shit fight.

As two young boys from her mob stand arguing, LEAH moves between characters.

THE BOYS   She look deadly, eh?
She look better than deadly, she's solid!
That's *my* sister.
That's not your sister!
Yer she is, you don't know!
We go long way back...
Arrr where you meet her?
I met her in preschool.
Yeah?
Yeah!

STEFF   Racial harmony requires both parties to...[*yelling it up the back for the benefit of her mob*] SIT DOWN!...to negotiate...[*The fight continues*] They still goin' la...

Yelling up the back, completely ignoring the judges to whom she was giving the speech.

Hey u'fella, wanna knock off. Fuckin' sit down. U'fella makin' me fuckin' shame. I'll come up there and knock you down my fuckin' self...gorn [*They have stopped*]... good...

STEFF notices the impression she must have made on the judges and comes back to her senses.

There ya go racial harmony...[*winks*]

LEAH reaches into the garbage bags and pulls out the Miss Murgon sash.

LEAH   Steff was the first Black woman to win Miss Murgon.

To music she parades in slow motion: waving, handing out kisses and encouraging the audience to clap.

STEFF is then at home. There's a big party. LEAH plays all the characters, family, friends and boys. She moves around each character, standing on a different cow hide to define a change of characters. Moving around the punching bag to become the boys.

LEAH   Back home in the kitchen, party's jumping. Everybody's proud of Steff. The boys are boasting about their trophies. Big mob of women drinkin', laughin' and yarnin' up. Steff's big noting, talking up, getting pissed.

SISTER   Here, Steff, have a charge.
              Miss Murgon today, Miss World tomorrow.
              Hey you seen that Miss Tragic bitch's dress…gunnar, gunnar…poor thing.
              You want that dress eh, Steff?

STEFF is excited and a little pissed.

STEFF   Fuck that! Too short, no need. I don't want no dress showing my cheeks, shame job.

SISTER   You do!

THE BOYS I'm proud of my sister.
              Hey knock it off, don't fuckin' start.
              That's not your sister…you keep goin' and I'll punch cun' out of you.
              Yeah?
              What you gonna hit me with my brother?
              I hit you with this…

Combination punches.

> Come on cun' git up! Solid! Show me again now my
> brother but slow motion!

*As THE BOYS, LEAH repeats combination punches in slow motion, while
speaking in slow motion.*

> Come…on…get…up…cun'…

LEAH   This goes on all night.

The dialogue becomes rushed as the momentum of the party picks up.

BOY   Gorn, Aunty Flo, sing that song for us.

FLO   Hey, never mind about Aunty Flo, it's Mrs Murgon! Hip
              'em Jackson!

NANNA   Water…water

STEFF   SSSsshhh, thought I heard Daisy Duck…

SISTER   Here Steffie, do that one for us…

STEFF   [*Singing and dancing*] 'Everybody was kung fu fighting…'

BOYS   How'd you throw them punches, my brother?…Hey Mrs
              Murgon, give us a charge…

NANNA   Water, water.

SISTER   You want that dress, eh Steffie?

FLO   Come on bub, come dance with your mother.

LEAH dances. There is a long pause.

Then:

BOY   Eh, Steff…give us a kiss…

STEFF turns back to the bag (the boy) and takes off the dress. Pauses for a beat. Then hangs up the dress.

LEAH   For a couple of weeks Steff thought she was queen of the Wakka Wakka. Until her little secret got out.

SCENE 9   STEFF GOES WILD

STEFF is holding her yellow dress. Her brother grabs her by the hair and is pulling her across stage.

BROTHER   Myall little black bitch!

STEFF   Don't touch me, what are you looking at?

STEFF puts her yellow dress on.

FLO   Roddy, I said knock off!

LEAH   Shit's hit the fan. They're all there, going off, big noting. All the cars parked out the front of Mum's. Big meeting. Steff's on horns, scraped some fella.

FLO   [*To RODNEY*] Sit down. Roddy, knock it off. Everybody out, I said out! [*To STEFF*] Now, I hear that you're…sexually active.

STEFF   So! Why should it bother you what I do?
What about all the times when Dad would bring the booze around and you'd go, 'Hey, Steff, you wanna play a little game? You stay here and peel the labels off these bottles, we'll go and hide and when you're finished you can come and try and find us. Well you didn't worry about me then, did you? Even when I did find yas. You're the one who fuckin' taught me how to fuckin' fuck, fuck ya.
When I was cold, when I had to look after Nanna and after you. I was tired. People coming and going. Strange men. Telling them to fuck off so they wouldn't touch us.

STEFF (cont'd)   Me, keeping you breathing. I'm tired. Last bit of pension on grog. School to go to, tired. I'm so tired. Maybe its better if I wasn't around any more, eh! I'll kill myself... kill myself...I'll kill myself!

FLO   You do what you like, but you're grounded!

LEAH   Steff waited for hours to see if her mum'd come back and check. She never did. So that night Steff cut down to where her grandfather kept that pony, first time ever she took that pony and Steff went wild.

The drumming to 'Horse Hair' begins as LEAH throws a cow hide (STEFF's smaller hide) and it hits the stage. LEAH sings 'Horse Hair' while moving in a way that indicates sexuality, anger and the freedom of riding a horse.

LEAH   She cuts out of town, ridin' out through the high grass, out there by herself in the dark for a while, summer frock blowin', ridin' bare back, bolting, free of something. But back in town the pub is jumping. She gets some older boys to get her a couple of bottles of spumante, and now she's in the gutter, drinking through a straw. She's so pissed, but she's happy. [*As though drunk*] She cuts down to the church and now she's on her back looking up at the big tree. Boyfriend having a scrape. The leaves are whispering, 'Steff, Steff.' More grog...

STEFF   [*drunk*] I'm so fucked, I'm so fucked. But I gotta be at the Talent Quest, singing. I gotta sing.

LEAH   Her dress on back to front, nickers inside out. And then her cousin sees her.

Her cousin grabs her as if he's about to hit her.

BOY   Steffie, you drunk eh!

STEFF   Don't hit me! Don't hit me! I gotta sing.

LEAH   Then it's her turn, she makes her way up to the stage.

She looks out into the audience. There is a long pause as if she's trying to work out where she is and get her act together. Her love of music and desire to sing help her focus.

    And she sang…

STEFF sings 'Till There Was You', a capella, in a fragile voice.

    'There were bells on a hill'

Letting the missing words from the song hang in the air, LEAH takes off STEFF's yellow dress, which has been synonymous with childhood, and hangs it up.

    'but I never heard them ringing…'

She continues to sing to the end of the verse.

SCENE 10   GOING SHOPPING

Physicalise driving the Datsun Sunny, while singing...

LEAH   '*Sunny, gees I'm getting sick of singing this song*'...
            fuckin' AM radio...
            When I arrived in Sydney, I was offered the job on the
            cable TV and they took one look at my clothes, gave me
            a stylist, an American Express card and said, 'Go
            shopping'...
            I thought about it for two seconds and went '*Alright!*'

*LEAH picks up a garbage bag, twists it around and throws it with a thump
on the stage.*

            Up'ome'der shopping was different for us [*thump*] there'd
            be a thump on the verandah. 'Thanks, St Vinnie's.' Mum
            would yell, 'Let's go shopping!' [*Looking through the bag.*]
            We go for the good stuff, we had our dignity. Then we'd
            chuck the bag on a friend's verandah down the road
            [*thud*] and so on down the street [*thump*]. Later you'd see
            a kid wearing the garbage bag with the corners cut out.
            Gunnar, gunnar...They really poor, eh.
            Being taken shopping with my own stylist is something
            pretty special. She took me up and down Oxford Street,
            Crown Street, and I'm trying on all these gorgeous
            clothes trying to feel like a *real* woman. Then I look at
            the prices. [*Mouths 'Fuck'*]
            I'll take it, they're buyin'. And you know what she got
            me?

*As LEAH talks, she pulls clothes from a garbage bag. They are white
meatworker's clothes.*

LEAH (cont'd)   She got me a lovely little cropped jacket from Chanel [*white industrial coat*], a gorgeous little hat from Armani [*hair net*], a pair of beautiful little blue trousers from Bracewell [*white trousers*], a lovely pair of purple high-heel shoes, with the crimson soles and the crimson lining from Lisa Ho [*white gumboots*].

She walks like a model.

And didn't little 'Leah Purcell' look grand.

She walks around the punching bag to the meatworks.

SCENE 11   MEAT

Music: rhythmic industrial sounds. Hydraulics, pumps etc, form a soundscape.

LEAH walks around to the hides upstage.

LEAH   Slaughter house.
6 am start.
Steff'd try to get work there along with everyone else.
Foreman had to choose you. You had to walk past the pens. They stank. She could hear the cattle fretting.
They'd smell the blood.

LEAH steps from one cow hide to another as she says a line for each cow.

COWS   [1:] Where they taking us, Daisy?
[2:] Moo, gonna slaughter us I bet.
[3:] Moooo, knock off, we'll be back.
[2:] You thick or what? They're taking us away.
[3:] You going fuckin' womba, why they feed us up so good if they don't want us.
[4:] Moo, I want my mummy.
[1:] Oh gunnar, gunnar, don't cry little fella, they got better homes for us and a new mother too.
[2:] Bullshit, you gonna be rump steak bub, run.
[3:] Whitefella wouldn't do that. What's all that blood.

To the sound of a stun gun, as part of the soundscape, she shoots one of the cows, there is a pause in the soundscape and it starts again.

LEAH physicalises a packing room as she talks. Every action is repetitive and methodical. Placing pieces of meat in boxes, closing the boxes and pushing them along a conveyor belt.

LEAH   Steff's first day. Women packing. Conveyor belt. [*Action: boxing meat*] Basically packing, shrink-wrapping and boxing up meat.

WOMAN   Shut your mouth, love, you'll catch a fly. Now your place is over here.
             Hey, Doreen! Have you met 'Jedda'? Wonder how long this one will last?
             You know what you're looking for, Jedda? Briskett, flank and shoulder. You'll be right, just make sure it's dead.

LEAH looks up at a window above the packing room as she talks.

LEAH   The men from the slaughter house would look down through a blood-splattered window to see who was working. They called:

BLOKES   Eh come and look! New blood on the floor!

STEFF is startled by all that is going on around her.

WOMAN   Who's meat's this? Are you with us Jedda, this ain't no bloody dreamtime, you know. S'pose you'll go bloody walkabout on us soon, eh?

STEFF   It's so cold…the smell…the blood…I'm tired…I'm so tired.

STEFF runs out to vomit.

FOREMAN Steffie, what are you doing out here?

STEFF   Sorry, sir.

FOREMAN   It's alright, alright. I wanted to talk to you anyway. Now
            when you've finished school, I won't be giving you a job
            here. Do you know why? I saw you in the Talent Quest.
            You can be anything you want, girlie. So don't come
            running to me looking for a job.

STEFF   Great. Anything I want…like unemployed.

LEAH takes off the meatworker's clothes and hangs them up.

SCENE 12   FUNERAL

LEAH hangs up her mother's frock carefully and then takes a long black dress from one of the green garbage bags and holds it as she begins singing. She then slips it on slowly as she continues the song and moves upstage to the last of the hides. It is beautiful—large, luscious and cream. She sits upstage and holds it over her leg, caressing it, as she sings 'Beautiful Day' by Bob Neuworth.

LEAH   *When I first heard the news that you were going down*
             It did not make me feel that well
             In my heart I knew that
             you were heaven bound.
             Having done your time down here in hell.

             And then this morning at the breaking of dawn I swear
             I heard the closing of a door
             Though in my heart I knew another had opened
             The way it had done so many times before.

             What a beautiful day to go to heaven
             Oh what a day to hear a red bird sing.
             What a wonderful way to go to Heaven
             Carried by Angels born to meet the king.

LEAH throws the cream hide and steps onto it. The movement during this dialogue is highly stylised, choreographed between CLIFFORD's hide and FLO's.

LEAH   Steff's mum had a brother-in-law, Clifford,
             old man could've been a great man. People said he was
             womba. Went bush, drank, old drone. But something in
             him would rise out of the grog haze, and he'd know
             himself.

LEAH (cont'd)   Steff was a bit scared of Uncle Cliffy, because when he
                walked you couldn't hear him.
                One morning, he came silently at dawn.

*The movement is between the two hides, creating a sense of mystery
and power: hands, feet, dust, silence, dignity, the early morning, and a
bottle of port.*

CLIFFORD   Florence.

FLO   What's that? Who that?

CLIFFORD   Florence, it is I, Clifford. Do you mind if I sit on your
            verandah and watch the sun come up?

FLO   Nah, gorn then.

LEAH   There'd be a rustle of paper and crack of a metal lid.

FLO   Here, Cliffy, what, you drinking?

CLIFFORD   A fine bottle of port, my sister, a fine bottle of port.

FLO   Cliffy, my legs.

CLIFFORD   That's why I'm here.

FLO   Bullshit, you got nowhere else to drink.
            Cliffy, I can't taste this.

CLIFFORD   That's right, my sister. You dying.

FLO   Well you better gimme some more of that grog.

LEAH begins to dance traditional movements as she speaks. These movements continue throughout this scene, building in intensity and changing when FLO speaks.

LEAH   She took her time dying. All the sisters, all brothers, all the mob sat around waiting for weeks. Every now and then she'd wake up and see our long faces and she'd yell:

FLO   Gorn get! I'm not fuckin' dead yet ya pack of vultures!

LEAH   Sorry, Mum.
Steff and them all snuck off good as gold to the kitchen. The sisters started cleaning up, sneaking around, picking up all the things that she had hoarded over the years, getting ready to chuck 'em. But Aunty Flo would hear them.

FLO   You leave all my stuff alone, I'm not fuckin' dead yet!

LEAH   Sorry, Mum.
The boys'd be in the kitchen, drinking, arguing over who won which trophies and she'd yell:

FLO   Hey? They're my trophies, u'fella only sell 'em for grog anyway. And I don't want any of them bastards mourning out those fuckin' songs in church either. Don't let them drag them out. I don't want them women wailing over the top. You make it real flash, Elvis Presley 'Inspiration'. I want 'Amazing Grace' coming in, 'Lead Me' when they're taking me out, and 'How Great Thou fucking Art' when they're putting me into the ground.

LEAH   She was a Christian lady.

FLO   And I don't want them bastards throwin' dirt on my
                coffin either, they been doing that all my life. I want fresh
                gum tips, new leaves from an old tree.
                Come here, Steff, bring baby Jess. Don't you cry for me,
                'cause once you're dead, you're a long time dead.
                Without you, bub, I would have been in the gutter. All
                the stuff in this house, it's yours. You can get away now,
                fly away, Bungabura.

*Music under: 'Amazing Grace' sung by Elvis Presley. The hides are
collected and rolled up, forming a large shape reminiscent of a body
made of skin.*

*The projection of the elder's eyes from 'Run Daisy Run' gradually fades
in upstage.*

STEFF   Mum…Mum…you breathin'?

*STEFF places young gum tips across the wrapped-up body of her mother
upstage. She then walks around the punching bag and stands as if
looking at what is left of her mother's life.*

STEFF   Four busted toasters, two broken blenders, plastic
                flowers, buttons, zips, elastic, old photos, newspaper
                clippings, mats, rugs.

*LEAH walks back to the rolled-up hides and holds a dance pose until the
music ends.*

SCENE 13   FACE

Walking fast, LEAH moves to the punching bag and begins working it.

LEAH   Steff'd box. Like a boy, in silks. Great technique, her
            dad'd say, 'If only you were a boy, Australian Champion.'
            But she didn't want trophies, she wanted protection.
            Steff's party. Same house, Mum's gone. Nanna's gone.
            Grandfather's gone. Her daughter's older. Boyfriend
            moved in. Big party. Everyone's either gone home or
            flaked out, he's got her in the back room, shouting at
            her. Jess is curled up in the hall listening. She's tired.

BOYFRIEND Come 'ere bitch!

*Her BOYFRIEND (represented by the punching bag) pulls her towards him,
she pushes him off*

STEFF   Don't!

STEFF pulls away.

BOYFRIEND Come here, fuck ya!

He pulls her in again.

STEFF   Stop it!

Again she pulls away, pushing him off.

BOYFRIEND Come here.

The bag is pushed, swinging a long way out.

STEFF   Fuck off, leave me alone, don't you ever...

The bag swings back and hits her, lifting her. The bag has become the boyfriend. STEFF holds herself in close to the bag. She is being punched by the BOYFRIEND, between each line.

BOYFRIEND You being a smart bitch [*punch*], big notin' your fucking self [*punch*], little pretty bitch [*punch*], pretty bitch [*punch*].

The BOYFRIEND hits her, knocks her to the ground. As he yells he tries to get to her face. She hides it from him, protecting herself.

BOYFRIEND Give us your face…give us your face…I said give us your face…give us your face!

It dies down, he has obviously left. STEFF lays there, and then slowly sits up. The bag is swinging menacingly nearby.

LEAH   There's a little girl in the hallway. She's crying. She thinks her mummy is dead.

STEFF   Jess…ssshhh…Jess…Jess, come here bub.

STEFF picks up hide as JESS.

          Don't cry baby…have a story eh? Just you and me. We're bare back, riding out from the showgrounds through high grass, just you an' me, eh. Our pony is all lathered, hang on tight. Grass whipping our ankles. Riding out under the grey old gum trees, bark hanging. Just you and me. Way out, we could lie down, flat on that grass the colour of mustard, under our big blue Queensland sky. And we can talk, eh. Say nothing. Just you an' me.
          Jess ssshhh. He's gone now. Oh Jess, Mummy's so tired. You're gonna have to help me, bub. Help me, Jess, please.

STEFF (cont'd)   I'm so sorry, I'm so sorry. Do you forgive Mummy?
                      It's happening all over again. Me and Mum.
                      There's no way out.

STEFF lies down slowly, with sore ribs, with the hide.

                      Oh Jess, Mummy's tired, I'm so tired…Come on bub,
                      put Mum to bed. Get in bed with Mum. Oh don't kick,
                      Jess, that's Mama's ribs.
                      If we sleep, we die. Come on, bub, we gotta go.
                      No more drinking.

*STEFF looks up at the punching bag which is still swinging slowly, and
cowers away.*

LEAH   Steff packed her things in garbage bags while he was
                      sleeping it off.
                      She rolls the car down the drive, quiet.
                      But there on the lawn are these blue cranes.
                      They're there for her. 'Fly away, fly away, Bungabura,
                      fly away.'

The industrial sounds from STEFF's meatworks' job are heard under.

                      Hide out…couple of days tops…petrol money and she's
                      off.

SCENE 14 BOXING

The industrial soundscape continues under.

Physicalise the boxing of meat on the conveyor belt, throughout the scene. Establish the window above.

LEAH   'Meat coming down'…Steff's packing, doing overtime.
        Up at the window, the boyfriend's there, sees her, he's laughing.
        The cattle's restless, trucks backing in…meat's real fresh …she's boxing.
        But something's braying like it's stuck…then the stun gun…then nothing. The compressors, the thud of carcass. All day the meat been coming down. Then it's not right…she's yelling…'It's too bloody'…coming down the conveyor…she's boxing it, but it's not right.
        Then up at the window…Steff's man's there…holding something…laughing…Holding up a mane…the neck of a pony…with its ears torn off.

STEFF   Look at the pony…the meat…look at the fucking meat …in the boxes!
        There's no way out…there's no way out…

Scene 15   ROAD KILL

Over near the blue mat, STEFF is in the car about to drive. There is choreographed traditional dancing and the driving of the car.

STEFF   Come on Jess, get in the car…see that tree on the bend …that's our tree.

LEAH   Steff guns the Datsun. Jess is in the front. She's giggling…It's a special treat. No seat belts.

LEAH is dancing. Choreographed traditional dance movements.

STEFF   Here bub, on Mum's lap…see that big old gum tree.
I'm going to crush Jess between my body and the steering wheel, so she's dead first, my little one.
But by the side of the car, galloping, is grandfather's pony.
Steff's there, summer frock blowin', riding him bare back. He's bolting, lathered, his eyes rolling. They're heading out through the high grass, under the great big blue Queensland sky. Steff will be riding him forever… up'ome'der.

Brolga dance, flying off and coming to a stop.

I'm slowing…the car's slowing…Jess is clapping, giggling…it's fun.
Should've been wrapped around that tree.
Fucking pony saved me.
Come on, Jess, click clack front and back, gorn.
We've finished that now.

LEAH sings while driving out from up'ome'der.

LEAH   'Bare faced and bare feet and bare back, don't take me
              back there.'

LEAH *walks over to the bench, casually whistling the bridge from 'Horse
Hair' and sits down.*

LEAH   [*whistling*] 'Bare skinned and lay bare, bare back, don't
              take me back there.'

LEAH *walks to the wooden bench whistling the same melody, and sits
down.*

SCENE 16   LEAVING

LEAH sits on bench very relaxed and looks around.

LEAH   So here we are in [*name of local city*] Solid eh? There's
             some suits in tonight. Producers and directors...They
             want me. Well I hope they want me...but they might be
             racist. [*To same brothers up the back*] ''Ere my brothers!'
             [*punching action*]

LEAH looks around at the crowd, trying to locate the suits.

             So where are youse? [*Looking into crowd*]
             So what can I do for you?

LEAH stands up in front of the bench.

             A bit of this? [*Does a traditional dance: Ngurrinynarmi*]
             Too Black?

*She thinks for a moment and then sings in a very white voice, with white
choreography, one line from a patriotic Australian advertising jingle.*

             Too White?

Walking to centre stage, she has an idea.

             'Everybody was Kung Fu Fighting...'
             Ah whatever.

Having reached the blue mat.

             Year 2000 Olympics...the eyes of the World will be
             upon us.
             Bring 'em out.

Leah stands in the traditional pose of man with spear, shading eyes.

Remember when I told you about the lovely Chanel jacket and the beautiful Bracewell blue trousers and the lovely Lisa Ho purple high-heel shoes with the crimson soles and the crimson lining?

Well at the cable TV launch I took them off…one at a time! The suits are all there. [*face action: mouth is hanging open*] I take them clothes and I throw them at them… and 'fuck-me-'rone', they start fighting over my clothes, tearin' at 'em, pullin' at 'em and they won't let go. Then they start pullin' each other around in a circle, around and around, faster and faster, thicker and thicker…and then all of a sudden they're gone

and all that's left is a great big pool of…

Viagra!

To the audience.

So here, just watch your step on the way out. OK, cuss!

Leah returns to working the bag. With the music to 'I'm Free' under.

Fade.

Traditional Language

Barambah: 'Where the water ripples'. The name given to the Aboriginal settlement where Leah Purcell's family were placed. Now known as Cherbourg.
Bidjarri: my grandmother's tribe of south-west Queensland
buba: father
bungabura: blue crane
corroboree: traditional dance
Gamilaroi: northern New South Wales tribe
gubba: New South Wales term for white person.
gundaburri: pregnant
gunnar: like 'poor person', to feel sorry
gunung: shit
joujin: child/children
Koori: New South Wales blackfella
migloo: Queensland term for white person
Murri: Queensland blackfella
myall: description the white settlers used for the blacks. Murri people use it to mean being shy.
ngumba: mother
Ngurrinynarmi: traditional dance of the re-enactment of the Bunya feast
Nunga: South Australian blackfella
Nyoongar: West Australian blackfella
Palawa: Tasmanian blackfella
tidda: sister

tulla: where
Wakka Wakka: tribe of the Cherbourg area in south-west Queensland
witalow: Black woman
womba: crazy
yani: cry
yumba: house

MURRI ENGLISH

big notin': trying to be the centre of attention
Blue Nurses: health nurses, their uniforms are blue
bullimen/bossmen: men of authority, such as the police or
    superintendent
charge: drink alcohol
clocked: hold eye contact seriously
come on, stuck right in, balls an' all: sexual expression used by young
    people
country: everybody
cuss: friendly term for your mate, cousin or other relation
deadly: excellent
feed: a meal
flatten ya': knock you out.
gin jockey: whiteman who liked Black woman solely for sex
gorn: go on
hip hip'em Jackson: Leah's mother's expression, it was to emphasise
    what she had just said, or to express her happiness
Jackson: nickname Leah's mother called anybody and everybody
knock off: stop it
la: to emphasise the sentence or phrase that precedes it
mission: an Aboriginal settlement run by a white superintendent, or
    by a church group. Authorities forced Aboriginal people to live
    on the missions.

mob: a general term to describe a large group of people, including
    your family; for example, 'That's my mob'

muck up: playing up badly

my shout: to offer to pay for a round of drinks

on horns: sexually aroused

punt cun' out of ya: punch cunt out of you

real flash: very nice

scrape/scraped: had sexual intercourse

shame: embarrassment, 'I couldn't possibly do that'

solid: pretty good

top, middle and bottom camps: where the different tribal groups set
    up their camp areas on the mission

true's god: fair dinkum

u'fellas: you fellows

up'ome'der: up home there

yarnin' up: to talk up big

Notes to the Play

Robyn Sheahan-Bright

'You one of my mob, eh?' This play invites the audience into the world of Leah Purcell, Aboriginal woman, mother, sister, daughter, actor, singer and activist. It's a journey through the highs and lows of a talented young person's life and through some of the challenges that face women, and also Aboriginal people, today. Scott Rankin and Leah Purcell's script is about strength and sheer feistiness. It's about pride and resilience. It's about a woman's love of performance, and of telling stories to explain away life's cares. This is an elegy to the spirit, to the triumph of will over circumstance. 'Deadly!' is the best word to describe the action in this play. Leah Purcell refuses to let anyone box her in. She wants to be free.

THEMES

Survival and Inner Strength

'There's no way out…there's no way out!' (Scene 14) Leah has had some hard knocks in her life, but she doesn't moan about them. She sends herself up and makes her audience see the funny side; a powerful way to engage their interest. In this roller-coaster, re-telling of her life she follows 'Steff' from a difficult upbringing in Murgon, to a nearly disastrous young adulthood, and then to a triumphant later

life as Leah, an acclaimed performer. From a world in which your
fists are your only defence she traces a girl's determined fight to free
herself from a seemingly prescribed future. The fact of her
womanhood is one of the things that gives her strength. 'But the men
and the women would fight differently. With the men it was all piss
and wind. But with the women, they wouldn't say a word…they just
clock ya, dress tucked up in the undies…and it was on.' (Scene 1)
The word 'box' is used in two ways in the play: 'to fight' and 'to
package something', such as meat, for shipping out. The final crucial
scene determines that Leah will not be boxed up; instead she's going
to fight her way out. 'I come from a long line of champions.' (Scene 1)

Questions   What does boxing signify in this play?
               What gives Leah her strength?

Escape

'*Bare face and bare feet and bare back, don't take me back there.*'
(Scene 6) Various motifs of escape feature in the play, cementing the
central idea that Leah manages to elude the life which seemed to be
mapped out for her. For Steff (Leah), boxing, singing and later her
career take her away from the problems of her present and her past
life. For Florence, sources of temporary comfort and release are music
and alcohol, and for Daisy, they are memories. The rural landscape
acts as metaphor for escape as Leah regards riding the pony over the
land as a source of release: '*whipping grass on my ankles, wind in
my mouth…your hooves take me bolting into the bluest sky.*' (Scene
6) Despite its physical harshness, the outback gives these characters
strength. It matches their own uncompromisingly independent spirits.
Ironically, the city also becomes a symbol of escape when Leah makes
a new life there.

Questions   What might have happened to Leah if she didn't make
               the move?

> Why did the playwrights create the character of Steff to
> represent Leah in her earlier life?

Women

The strong women whose lives are depicted in this play all face
challenges, evincing tremendous fortitude, and becoming the mainstay
of their families. Daisy, Florence and Steff (Leah) represent three
generations of tough survivors. Florence is a powerful force—a big
woman of immense dignity and charm. Though drink creates
problems for her family, she dies with her pride intact: 'And I don't
want them bastards throwin' dirt on my coffin either, they been doing
that all my life.' (Scene 12) The constraints placed on women by
unequal opportunity and male expectations are explored here through
Steff's upbringing as a child often left to care for both her nanna and
her mother, Florence, and her later teenage pregnancy. Her mother's
death leads Steff into a similar pattern. In trying to escape her abusive
boyfriend, who used her as a punching bag, she briefly contemplated
killing herself and her daughter Jess. Happily, she escaped her fate
and became a successful actor and mother. She saved herself and
achieved her own potential.

The tradition of the woman speaking out for her own interests
has been developed by Australian writer–performers, including Robyn
Archer, Jean Kitson, Wendy Harmer and Gretel Killeen; satirists such
as Kaz Cooke and Lily Brett; and plays like *Radiance* and *Hotel
Sorrento*. They all speak directly to women, celebrating their triumphs,
and reflecting their concerns. Leah Purcell's life story is representative
of this tradition, and implies that her daughter will presumably inherit
the strength of the generations which precede her. In addition, this
play looks at the strength in us all—woman or man—and the power
of hope and self-esteem.

Question   Where do women glean their inner strength from in this
               play?

Tribes and Mobs: Family Relationships and Kinship

'OK cuss!' (Scene 16) The Aboriginal concept of an extended network of family and kin is given a wider application here as the play continually invites the entire audience, black or white, to come into Leah's great big 'family'. Notions of Aboriginal kinship are also sometimes extended in a flippant way to include whitefellas: 'Nar only jokin', cuss. So where you from and who your mob? You're not Murri, not Koori, Nyoongar, Nunga, Palawa...Woollahra. That explains it.' (Scene 1)

Activity   Find out more about the traditional groups and their country; for example, Wakka Wakka, Murri, Koori, Nyoongar, Nunga, Palawa.

Symbols

'Steff was Bungabura. When she was little her nanna called her that, Gamilaroi for blue crane...' (Scene 4) Leah's nanna sees that Leah is elegant and lithe like the blue crane, which becomes a powerful symbol in this play. ('Bungabura' is Leah's totem.) It is a family totem—birds, air, spiritual guide 'Bunjil'. When Nanna tells Steff she is a bungabura she implies that Steff will fly away, before she is caught in the sort of trap which ensnared her mother. She has a spiritual insight in recognising that Steff has the capacity to escape.

Steff draws most of her inspiration from the pony; the image of her riding with her hair blowing free is one that features in many women's dreams—black or white. This powerful image is the force that both leads Steff to the brink of despair and suicide, and which saves her. When she discovers that the meat she has been boxing up is horse-meat, she is nearly driven crazy with disgust and sadness. Confronted with the concept of 'pure evil'— her boyfriend's deliberate slaughtering of the animal that he knows she loves, her grandfather's pony—she sees the destruction of a childhood dream that has always given her hope. Steff takes a wild drive with her daughter Jess, intending to run the car into the tree—the one under which she had the 'scrape' with her boyfriend. Then she sees the spirit of the younger Steff riding that horse, and she has a moment of rare spiritual awakening. The pony racing beside the car reminds her of her dreams and restores her strength. She breaks away and heads for a new life.

Cow hides are another symbolic feature of the play. Throughout the performance, Leah uses cow hides to denote the characters as she introduces them. Their significance is developed further in reference to the meatworks in Murgon, where girls like Steff are employed. When the animals are being herded for the killing floor, they speak to each other: 'cows: 1. Where they taking us, Daisy? 2. Moo, gonna slaughter us I bet.' (Scene 11) The use here of the name Daisy, heard earlier in the song about Steff's nanna and other children being herded up and taken away from their parents, is clear. The symbolism is developed further when the blokes see the women starting work at the meatworks: 'Eh come and look! New blood on the floor!' (Scene 11) The cows are symbolic of people: 'Whitefella wouldn't do that' (Scene 11) says one cow to another. But of course whitefella has done worse than slaughter cows. He's also been responsible for killing many Aboriginal people.

Question   The pony has a spiritual significance for Steff. What do you think it represents?

Reconciliation

'Racial harmony requires both parties to...SIT DOWN!...to negotiate... They still goin' la... Hey u'fella, wanna knock off.' (Scene 8) Achieving racial harmony is not easy. This play shows, in humourous ways, how racism is expressed, and how often racial 'tolerance' is shallow or even hypocritical. Leah jokingly assumes the superior position as a way of subverting ingrained racism in patronising those who are used to assuming their own superiority. 'So now I live in Woollahra…which is nice…because as Aunty Pauline Hanson says, "Too many people up'ome get paid too much money for sitting around drinking too much port." So Woollahra feels like home.' (Scene 2) Leah's ability to be condescending gives her character strength. She invites the audience and readers to question themselves and to observe how those who purport to express 'inclusiveness', often betray themselves in their behaviour. The play also demonstrates the relationship between racial superiority and economic power in dramatic ways. For example, when Leah arrives at a real estate agent's office in Woollahra, in Sydney's Eastern Suburbs, her appearance makes the agent respond in panic: 'We haven't any money, we haven't any money, take whatever you want.' (Scene 2) Often people who express objections to those of other races are merely feeling insecure about their own positions.

Questions   Observe the practice of reconciliation in your community (for example, family, school, university, workplace). How, for instance, do people deal with racist jokes?
What does the term 'Reconciliation' actually mean?
What has the practice of enforced 'assimilation' denied to the Aboriginal people?

ASPECTS OF THE WRITING

Real Deadly Humour

Leah presents herself as an independent and wickedly entertaining character in a script written partly in the tradition of the stand-up comic. 'The boys got all the deadly things, the trophies, the Golden Gloves… The brain damage.' (Scene 1) Throughout the play Leah shows that she is capable of getting over difficult situations by laughing at them. She also highlights the reserve of urban dwellers compared with the rural tendency to be more open. For example, when she tries to tell her life story to someone sitting next to her on a bench in the city—'My father he's white, two wives... It gets better! I haven't got up to the part about me being conceived at the dump!' (Scene 2)— they respond by running away! Several other Indigenous performers, writers and artists also use humour. Herb Wharton's yarns are often self-deprecating: 'If Aboriginal people had got to the Garden of Eden first, they wouldn't have eaten the bloody apple, they'd have eaten the snake instead!' Ernie Dingo tells a joke that: 'The only time I wish I was white is at three o'clock in the morning trying to catch a cab.' (Coolwell, p. 82) Kev Carmody's songs and Mudrooroo's poems, such as the 'Giant Debbil Dingo', also laugh at misfortune.

Questions   Do you think humour is effective as a means of bringing about understanding?

Is it a universal means of communication?

Storytelling and Yarns

'And all that's left is this lovely cup of delicious yellow butter. And I'm thinkin', hey, this good food, can't be wastin', so I get stuck into it!' (Scene 7) Storytelling can help people to explore and deal with emotions, transforming even negative experiences into positive ones. For example, in Scene 7 the story of a white woman reacting to a black face with fear and distaste is translated into a kind of folk tale, with a distinct similarity, in a refracted form, to the classic tale 'Little Black Sambo'. Leah tries to reach out to the white woman to rescue her, is rejected, and ends by eating her instead, just as Sambo does the tigers. Leah's anger at the woman's reaction is re-directed into an imaginative exploration of her own feelings. This idea is again picked up at the end of the play when the greedy media all dissolve into a 'great big pool of Viagra!' (Scene 16)

Question   Which of the stories in the play do you find most interesting? Why?

Life Writing

'I'm from Queensland…up'ome'der…Joh's country…Murgo
Barambah Mission…Wakka Wakka Tribe…BIG family…' (Scen
Everyone has a life story to tell. It's just a question of how to appr
the telling. Often writers forget that the same principles apply to
writing as they do to any storytelling medium. They are: theme,
characterisation, style, readability, structure, marketability. Eve
story written only for your family must capture the readers' atten
and keep them enthralled throughout the telling.

Writers of the performance of a life story, such as Box the P
have even more elements to consider. Scott Rankin and Leah Pu
lead the audience through the play in an intimate way. Also, Box
Pony is political without being didactic. Leah adopts a caring appr
to her largely white audience, inviting their friendship rather
accusing them or making them feel uncomfortable. Above all,
writers understand that the play has to 'work' as an entertair
'high-octane' piece of theatre.

A life story may be told through a variety of genres: autobiogra
biography, play, film, novel, poem, or song. Box the Pony, for exan
is a complex mixture of autobiography, biography and yarns or
tales dramatising the major events in Leah Purcell's life. Leah n
fact with fiction in her yarns, as do other writers such as Lily
and Herb Wharton.

It can be written in several voices: the first, third or even se
person. This play appears to have been written in first person
an examination of the text shows that it is an inter-weaving of vo
first person—'I love working the bag' (Scene 1); third person—'S
play tricks on Nanna, like move her bedpan out of reach.' (Scen
and sometimes the second person—'What you lookin' at? You lo
at me?… You was.' (Scene 1)

A life story can also consist of a combination of different '
woven together by the writer, such as, poems, songs, news

clippings and prose. *Box the Pony* contains several different 'texts'. Factual accounts are interrupted by expository narratives; the dialogue is punctuated by songs illustrating some of the events that haunt the action; it has dramatic re-enactments in the voices of others, such as the cows speaking to each other in Scene 11; it contains mime and dance; it uses artefacts—including the landrights jumper, cow hides, the dresses representing the characters, and the meatworker's uniform—to denote or represent various themes and to achieve dramatic effect.

A writer may choose to weave together more than one person's life story. This play gives us some of the lives of Florence and Daisy too, though it is primarily Steff's (Leah's) story. Rita Huggins and Jackie Huggins' *Auntie Rita* is an example of a book written in two voices, as is James McBride's *The Color of Water*.

In *Box the Pony* there is also a deliberate element of fiction. By using the fictional character of 'Steff', the writers can tell Leah's story while helping the audience to become involved in the play. They have elaborated on the themes of Leah's life to make the metaphors more powerful.

Choosing the order of events and the structure of the work is often crucial when writing a life story. A chronological order may not be the most effective way to capture the reader's interest. *Box the Pony* moves between the present and past, using flashbacks to demonstrate how Leah finds herself on the stage, and to detail the lives of members of her family.

Some of the most successful life stories are about ordinary people, such as *A Fortunate Life* by A. B. Facey or *Angela's Ashes* by Frank McCourt, who do not achieve anything outstanding. Also, social history, which looks at the way ordinary people live their lives, can be more revealing and engaging than traditional historical approaches, which examine momentous events or periods.

Women's stories often concentrate on the domestic sphere and on relationships rather than on events or achievements. Some women's lives have been largely undocumented and writers have had to construct 'fictional biographies', such as Brian Matthews' *Louisa*, or biographical novels including Anne Brooksbanks' *All My Love*. Many Indigenous women are now recording their own life stories. Joy Hooton writes that: 'No document has a greater chance of challenging the cult of forgetfulness than a black woman's autobiography.' (1990, p. 313) Leah Purcell and Scott Rankin have added to that tradition in writing a genuine Aboriginal women's story which could be any woman's story.

Another issue for a life writer is to decide what to leave out. What events are key to understanding the person? Who were the important people in their life? How might their life have been lived differently? In theatrical terms, what was 'left out' also gave structure, thematic strength and dramatic power to *Box the Pony*.

Writing this play was a collaborative process between Scott Rankin and Leah Purcell. To successfully work with another writer involves a lot of listening, and the ability to compromise. Both writers agree that their differences gave the piece its strength, and its relevance to a wide audience.

Questions   Would you like to have read more about any of the characters mentioned in *Box the Pony*? For example, Cliffie or Steff's grandfather.

Do you think the writers deliberately wrote about women characters rather than men. Why?

What might the pitfalls and strengths have been in a white man and a black woman co-authoring a play?

Is this life story a way of discussing 'bigger' issues?

Is it a play about Aboriginal issues or is it just as much about escape?

Activity   Write a list of three things that happened in your childhood which you consider important. Choose one of them and tell the story, in about 1000 words.

OTHER TOPICS

Missions and Government Reserves

'"Mission" is a term loosely used for various Aboriginal and Torres Stait Islander reserves and government stations as well as Christian institutions.' (Horton, p. 706) Leah grew up in Murgon, near Barambah reserve, an Aboriginal settlement that was established in 1906, and renamed Cherbourg in 1931. Many of the residents of nearby Durundur, a temporary reserve, were transferred to Barambah in 1903. In the early days the people forcibly removed to Barambah had few rights. The government, for instance, regularly 'extracted "contributions" from the wages of employed Aborigines living on its settlements, and sold settlement produce'. (Kidd, p. 64) Conditions were poor, and 'Inadequate government funding took an unremitting toll on Aboriginal health'. (Kidd, p. 63) In the ensuing decades many injustices were perpetrated, and the Aboriginal people, particularly after the 1960s, began to campaign for better conditions. Tragically, 'There is little doubt that the post-1971 availability of alcohol on the previously dry communities caused turmoil.' (Kidd, p. 302) Cherbourg has since developed a strong culture as a Murri-controlled community with its own businesses, including cattle operations and an emu farm. Several other prominent Indigenous artists came from there, including Harold Blair, Maroochy Barambah and Lionel Fogarty. Leah grew up in an unusual situation: her white father had two families, one white and one black, both of which lived in Murgon, not on the mission. So Leah was caught between two worlds—black and white.

Question   How does society treat children of mixed parentage?

Activity   Find out what you can about missions in the various states of Australia.

Stolen Children

In the song 'Run Daisy Run', Leah tells the story of her grandmother
being forcibly removed from her people and taken to a mission. It's
a shock to discover that even recently white authorities were still
taking Aboriginal children away from their families. The play is set
between 1970 and the late eighties, though some stories, such as
Daisy's, took place earlier. The *1897 Aboriginals Protection and
Restriction of the Sale of Opium Act* gave the Queensland Government
the power to confine Indigenous people on missions and reserves. It
made the so-called 'chief protector the legal guardian of all Aboriginal
children'. (Horton, p. 914) Such legislation remained 'essentially the
same until 1984'. (Horton, p. 915) The tragedy incurred by this
legislation was compounded by the use of Aboriginal Native Police to
capture their own people, and is obliquely referred to in the play when
Steff mistakes her own grandfather, a drover, for 'One of them
Government blackfellas'. (Scene 4)

Activity   Read some of the stories of 'stolen children'.

Domestic and Alcohol Abuse

The cycle of substance abuse is a hard one to break, and often leads
to, or is caused by, violence in the home.

Question   How does Leah manage to break the cycle?

Teenage Self-esteem: Suicide and Emotional Problems

There are damning statistics which demonstrate that suicide is very
prevalent among young people in Australia. Writers for young people
have tackled the issue of self-esteem in imaginative ways in novels
such as Judith Clarke's *Night Train*, a marvellously evocative text about
the pressures of exams; *Deadly Unna!* by Philip Gwynne, a stirring
account of a boy overcoming his perceived problems via his friendship

with an Aboriginal boy; and Melina Marchetta's *Looking for Alibrandi*, which reflected Italo-Australian experiences.

Questions   Can writers show us ways to deal with teenage angst?

Individual and collective political action

There are many ways of expressing political opinions. For example, by overt means such as becoming involved in party politics, joining groups and organisations, or participating in collective responses to issues, including attending demonstrations and signing petitions. The less overt, more individual responses include those made by artists who often make 'political' points in artworks, books, or plays like this one.

Questions   What issues does this play address or refer to?
               Do you think the play is an effective means of conveying ideas?
               How has the storytelling tradition been a powerful political response to social issues?

Further Reading

Plays about Women

Archer, Robyn, *The Pack of Women*, Penguin, Ringwood, 1986.

Dean, Philip, *Long Gone Lonesome Cowgirls*, Currency Press, Sydney, 1995.

Mailman, Deborah and Enoch, Wesley, *The Seven Stages of Grieving*, Playlab Press, Brisbane, 1996.

Murray, Peta, *One Woman's Song*, commissioned by QTC, Brisbane, 1993.

Nowra, Louis, *Radiance*, Currency Press, Sydney, 1993.

Rayson, Hannie, *Hotel Sorrento*, Currency Press, Sydney, 1990.

Ryder, Sue, *Matilda Women*, Playlab Press, 1993.

Family and Social History

Dow, Gwyn and Factor, June, *Australian Childhood: An Anthology*, McPhee Gribble, Melbourne, 1991.

Hooton, Joy, *Stories of Herself When Young: Autobiographies of Childhood by Australian Women*, OUP, Melbourne, 1990.

Kociumbas, Jan, *Australian Childhood: A History*, Allen & Unwin, St Leonards, 1997.

Kyle, Noeline and King, Ron, *The Family History Writing Book*, Allen & Unwin, St Leonards, 1993.

Miller, Patti, *Writing Your Life*, Allen & Unwin, St Leonards, 1994.
Niall, Brenda and Britain, Ian, *Oxford Book of Australian School Days*, OUP, Melbourne, 1997.

Fiction

Brooksbank, Anne, *All My Love*, William Heinemann, Melbourne, 1991.
Clarke, Judith, *Night Train*, Penguin, Ringwood, 1997.
Franklin, Miles, *My Brilliant Career*, Angus & Robertson, Sydney, 1954, 1986.
Gwynne, Philip, *Deadly Unna!*, Penguin, Ringwood, 1998.
Marchetta, Melina, *Looking for Alibrandi*, Puffin, Ringwood, 1992.
Wharton, Herb, *Unbranded*, UQP, St Lucia, 1992.

Life Stories

Cochrane, Kathie, *Oodgeroo*, UQP, St Lucia, 1994.
Conway, Jill Ker, *The Road From Coorain*, Heinemann, Melbounre, 1989.
Coolwell, Wayne, *My Kind of People: Achievement, Identity and Aboriginality*, UQP, St Lucia, 1993.
Edmund, Mabel, *No Regrets*, UQP, St Lucia, 1992.
Facey, A.B., *A Fortunate Life*, Penguin, Ringwood, 1981.
Forte, Margaret, *Flight of an Eagle: the Dreaming of Ruby Hammond*, Wakefield, South Australia, 1995.
Henning, Rachel, *The Letters of Rachel Henning*, Penguin, Ringwood, 1963, 1988.
Houbein, Lolo, *Wrong Face in the Mirror: an Autobiography of Race and Identity*, UQP, St Lucia, 1990.
Huggins, Rita and Huggins, Jackie, *Auntie Rita*, Aboriginal Studies Press, Canberra, 1994.
Langford, Ruby Ginibi, *Don't Take Your Love to Town*, Penguin, Ringwood, 1988.
Langford, Ruby Ginibi, *My Bundjalung People*, UQP, St Lucia, 1994.
Lyden, Jackie, *Daughter of the Queen of Sheba*, Hodder Headline, Sydney, 1998.

McBride, James, *The Color of Water*, Hodder Headline, Sydney, 1997.

McCourt, Frank, *Angela's Ashes*, Scribner, New York, 1996.

McDonald, Connie Nungalla (with Jill Finnane), *When You Grow Up*, Magabala, Broome, 1996.

Matthews, Brian, *Louisa*, McPhee Gribble, Melbourne,1987.

Morgan, Sally, *My Place*, Fremantle Arts Centre Press, Fremantle, 1987.

O'Faolain, Nuala, *Are You Somebody? The Life and Times of Nuala O'Faolain*, Hodder Headline, Sydney, 1998.

Pryor, Boori (Monty), *Maybe Tomorrow*, Penguin, Ringwood, 1998.

Roughsey, Elsie, *An Aboriginal Mother Tells of the Old and the New*, McPhee Gribble/Penguin, Ringwood, 1984.

Sayer, Mandy, *Dreamtime Alice*, Random House Australia, Sydney, 1998.

Smith, Shirley and Sykes, Roberta, *Mum Shirl*, Heinemann Educational, Melbourne, 1981.

Sykes, Roberta, *Snake Cradle*, Allen & Unwin, St Leonards, 1998.

Tucker, Margaret, *If Everyone Cared*, Ure Smith, Sydney, 1977.

Utemorrah, Daisy and Torres, Pat, *Do Not Go Around the Edges*, Magabala, Broome, 1991

Walker, Kath (Oodgeroo), *Stradbroke Dreamtime*, Angus & Robertson, Sydney, 1972.

Ward, Glenyse, *Wandering Girl*, Magabala, Broome, 1987.

Aboriginal Culture

Children's Books:

Calley, Karin and Pearson, Noel, *Caden Wallaa*, Jam Roll/UQP, St Lucia, 1994.

Fogarty, Lionel and Hodgson, Sharon, *Booyooburra*, Hyland House, Melbourne, 1993.

Other Texts:

Bell, Diane, *Daughters of the Dreaming*, McPhee Gribble/Allen & Unwin, St Leonards, 1985.

Bird, Carmel (ed.), *The Stolen Children: Their Stories*, Random House Australia, Sydney, 1998.

'Bringing Them Home', Report of the National Inquiry into the Separation of Aboriginal and Torres Strait Islander Children from Their Families, April 1997.

Davies, Kerry (ed.), *Across Country: Stories from Aboriginal Australia*, ABC Books, Sydney, 1998.

Davis, Jack, et al, *Paperbark: a Collection of Black Australian Writings*, UQP, St Lucia, 1990.

Gilbert, Kevin (ed.), *Inside Black Australia: an Anthology of Aboriginal Poetry*, Penguin, Ringwood, 1988.

Horton, David, *The Encyclopaedia of Aboriginal Australia*, (2 vols) Aboriginal Studies Press, Canberra, 1994.

Kidd, Rosalind, *The Way We Civilise: Aboriginal Affairs, the Untold Story*, UQP, St Lucia, 1997.

Mudrooroo, *Indigenous Literature of Australia: Milli Milli Wangka*, Hyland House, Melbourne, 1997.

Reynolds, Henry, *Aboriginal Sovereignty*, Allen & Unwin, St Leonards, 1996.

Rintoul, Stuart, *The Wailing: a National Black Oral History*, Heinemann, Melbourne, 1993.

Shoemaker, Adam, *Black Words White Page: Aboriginal Literature 1929–1988*, UQP, 1989

Stanner, W.E.H., *After the Dreaming*, ABC, Sydney, 1969.

Reach Out

If you are experiencing or witnessing violence in families you can con

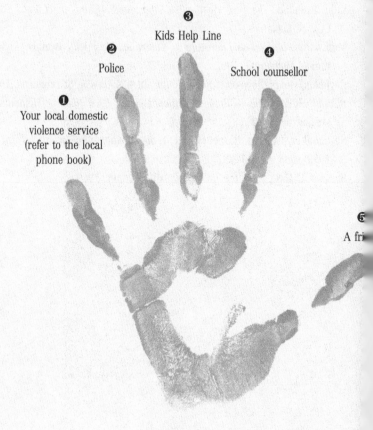

❸
Kids Help Line

❷
Police

❹
School counsellor

❶
Your local domestic
violence service
(refer to the local
phone book)

❺
A fri

BIG hART

In 1992 Scott Rankin co-foundered the organisation Big hART to work with people experiencing many of the issues captured in *Box The Pony*. Big hART's work with thousands of people experiencing severe disadvantage has taken them to over thirty communities across the country. During that time, the company has won many awards and been acknowledged as Australia's leading Arts and Social Change company.

Behind these many projects there has been one unifying theme, 'It's much harder to hurt someone if you know their story.' Through its projects, Big hART has provided assistance to those people forced to the outside of the community, helping them to gain the skills necessary to tell their story clearly, beautifully and professionally. In response, the community is encouraged to listen, understand and create opportunity for those on the outside, enabling them to re-enter the community and participate, and governments are encouraged to examine aspects of their social policy.

Over the years, the positive results of Big hART's projects has caught the eye of many, with seven awards from the heads of Australian governments, to those working at the grassroots.

Festival Director Robyn Archer puts it succinctly:

'Big hART has been working with outsider culture in Australia for a very long time, during which it has been the very model of community cultural development. The company has always insisted on the excellence of its product and the health and authenticity of its process and this combination has distinguished its practice as the very best of its kind...'

Since working together on *Box The Pony*, Leah has contributed to many Big hART projects, often involving people experiencing issues such as domestic violence. She also gives advice to the board on indigenous issues.

Perhaps as a result of *Box The Pony*, Scott has been invited to work in many more indigenous projects, such as Ngapartji Ngapartji, Riverland and Mimili. For more information go to:

www.ngapartji.org
www.bighart.org

Acknowledgments

Bungabura Productions and I would like to thank and acknowledge the many people without whose support and assistance *Box the Pony* probably would not have seen the light of day.

Sue Rider, the Artistic Director of La Boîte Theatre Company in Queensland, who sat down in 1995 and helped me with my application to the Australia Council for the Arts for a Fellowship Grant to enable me to concentrate full-time on getting *Box the Pony* from the wish list to the starting line. Christine Ferguson and Di Underwood, Project Officers with the Indigenous Unit of the Australia Council, were of tremendous assistance. I am also grateful to the members of the Indigenous Board of Directors, who sat on the selection panel and gave me their seal of approval as the recipient of the 1996 Fellowship Grant for Performing Arts. Other people who supported and encouraged me and Bungabura Productions to tell my story were Gavin Jones and the staff at Deadly Sounds Radio and *Deadly Vibe* magazine, Cathy Craigie and the staff at Koori Radio and Gadigal Information Services. Thanks to Liz Croll of Cercus Design for all her wonderful work and creativity in preparing the graphic designs and presentations for the play.

On a personal note there are some people I would like to thank. Mr and Mrs Woods, my Physical Education teachers at Murgon State High School, for taking an interest in me. Ian Perkins and Jane Atkins, although you didn't know it at the time, you were my first professional audition panel. You told me that what I had done in the play was something special, and when everyone else told me to get a real job you both told me to chase my dreams. I thank you for that. Uncle John, Aunty Gracie, Waverley, Mary, Naomi, Judith, John, Neil, and James Stanley, thank you so much for being there when I needed you, my second family. All my love from your neighbour, neighbour.

Bungabura Productions and I would like to thank the following people in particular for playing key roles in the play's evolution from commissioning to opening night performance and beyond. Wendy Blacklock and her staff at Performing Lines as the original producers of the play. Rhoda Roberts, the Artistic Director of the Festival of the Dreaming, for your absolute faith in me to produce the goods and come up with a play that you hoped would turn people around in the way they look at indigenous contemporary theatre.

Finally, Bungabura Productions and I would like to thank family, friends and fans who have supported me and *Box the Pony* from the beginning. Thank you for your love and encouragement, it has meant more than you can imagine. To all those who crossed my path, for the good or the bad; without those encounters my story would not be so. To my little chicken, my daughter Manda Moon, Mama luvs ya! Thanks to the Ancient Spiritual Ancestors for their blessings and guidance, 'Alcheringa ngai yirri Baiame'.

Leah Purcell